APACHE AMBUSH

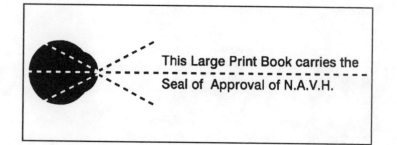

This Large Print Book carries the
Seal of Approval of N.A.V.H.

APACHE AMBUSH

CHET CUNNINGHAM

WHEELER PUBLISHING
An imprint of Thomson Gale, a part of The Thomson Corporation

Detroit • New York • San Francisco • New Haven, Conn. • Waterville, Maine • London

THOMSON
GALE

LIBRARY OF CONGRESS CATALOGING-IN-PUBLICATION DATA

Cunningham, Chet.
    Apache ambush / by Chet Cunningham.
        p. cm. — (Chisolm series) (Wheeler Publishing large print western)
    ISBN 1-59722-381-6 (alk. paper)
    1. Large type books. I. Title.
PS3553.U468A84 2006
813'.54—dc22   2006029848

U.S. Hardcover:
ISBN 13: 978-1-59722-381-2
ISBN 10: 1-59722-381-6

12/06 Thom. Gale 22.95 LT FIC CUNNINGHAM

Published in 2006 by arrangement with Chet Cunningham.

Printed in the United States of America on permanent paper
10 9 8 7 6 5 4 3 2 1

APACHE AMBUSH

CHAPTER 1
RAIDERS AT NOONTIME

The tall, lean man blended into the shadows as if he were a part of them, watching. Nothing moved. A dog howled in pain on the other side of the barn. The adobe house lay gutted, its thatched roof and cactus pole rafters still burning in the caldron formed by the thick walls that remained.

A hook-nosed hawk flapped down across the cactus pole corral, landing out of sight. This one was worse than the other Wade Chisolm had seen that morning. There was more death here, more anger. Even though he couldn't see any bodies, the tall man sensed them. No one had been left alive.

He ran effortlessly to the barn door and looked inside. A smoldering torch had fallen short of the loose hay and had not set the barn on fire. Just past the open door a man in overalls lay on his back, his throat gashed open, a bullet hole in his forehead. His hair was gone, exposing a red mass of bloody cranial bone and stringy tissue.

Across the man's legs lay a boy of a dozen years, his long yellow hair intact. Both his eyes had been gouged out, his front teeth broken inward. A lance had been thrust repeatedly into the boy's chest.

Chisolm frowned, stepped over the bodies and checked the barn. There were no horses or mules, as he had expected.

He ran to the remains of the house. He could see nothing but the smoldering poles and thatching. If there were any bodies in there they would remain. Behind the shell of the house near the well he found a girl of seventeen or eighteen. She was naked, her legs splayed apart, small angry burns on her breasts and stomach. One hand had been cut off and she had been scalped. The girl had not died quickly.

The tall man with the red hair and sharp features turned away from the carnage and trotted to the ravine that lay a quarter of a mile west of the house. There he mounted a broad-chested black, sitting easily in the army issue saddle. He walked the horse back toward the house, then leaned forward, watching the ground as he worked parallel to the buildings. He saw the smooth undulating track of a king snake in the dust, noticed how many beetle tracks had passed over it since it was made; soon discovered the tracks of a dozen or more horses, shod and unshod, moving toward the north.

After a half hour the tracks kept moving northward. On the next rise he looked ahead and saw a thin smoke from a kitchen fire. There was another ranch ahead and the hostiles were aiming for it. Chisolm put the black into an arroyo and rode hard now, hoping he could get there in time. He used every ravine, every wash, every bit of concealment he could find in the sparse, sun-baked Arizona wilderness.

Twenty minutes later, his sweating, heaving mount trembled as he tied him up to brush at the edge of a dry creek. Chisholm bent low and ran lightly on moccasined feet along the waterless stream bed toward a low ranch house. He carried with him an eight-pound Spencer repeating rifle. The big gun held seven copper, rim-fire cartridges, and one round could blast a hole two inches wide through a man's chest at 500 yards. He seldom went anywhere without his .52 calibre rifle.

At the end of the concealment he paused. The farm yard was just ahead, thirty yards from where he lay hidden. He saw no one, but he knew people were present. How many? He guessed about six from the hoofprints. Chisholm's dark eyes darted, evaluating one ambush point after another. He saw no hostiles.

They were there. What were they waiting for?

There was no sound behind him but he whirled, the rifle coming up to firing position. He had sensed the presence and now stared at an Apache fifteen feet away. The brave had a six-inch knife in his hand, and the other hand reached for his short bow looped over his back. The ambusher needed quiet, but noise made no difference to Chisholm.

"Another mighty Apache who stoops to slaughtering women and children because he is afraid to fight a man. What is your name, Baby Killer?" Chisholm had spoken the insult in Spanish, with occasional Apache words thrown in. Most of the Apache tribes spoke Spanish fluently because of their life on both sides of the border.

The brave, bare to the waist, wore buckskin leggings and moccasins. He grabbed the bow but Chisholm shook his head.

"No. You move that bow, Baby Killer, and I give you a fifty-two caliber lead bullet for your lunch."

The Apache shifted the knife to his right

hand and advanced slowly. Chisholm whipped his right hand to his left shoulder and drew a carefully shortened and sharpened Army sabre. The gleaming steel had been honed to a razorlike cutting edge. He stood the rifle against the tree and met the Indian's rush, slapping the short knife away to his left, lunged forward, and deftly sliced an inch-long gash in the Apache's left arm.

The hostile looked at the blood with surprise, then darted forward, feinted, spun around, and, in an unexpected movement, threw his knife. Chisholm saw the blade coming and lunged to the ground at the last moment to avoid the steel. As he got up he watched the Apache take advantage of the momentary diversion to race deeper into the thicket.

By the time Chisholm reached his rifle and sent one booming shot after the brave, he had vanished into the thicket of chaparrel. Chisholm turned and glanced at the farmyard. A man ran from the house a rifle in his hands.

"Back inside, you fool!" Chisholm bellowed. As his words died a rifle cracked from beyond the barn, but the bullet missed and the rancher dove back into his adobe fortress and slammed the door.

A voice floated to him from somewhere in

the line of brush.

"Longknife, today we will lift your worthless red scalplock."

Chisholm flattened behind the tree again and levered a new round into the firing chamber.

"You'll lift no hair unless it is a woman's or a roundeye baby, you eater of dog dung, you ancient squaw with no teeth."

Before the words were out of his mouth, Chisholm saw a lone brown form lift from the side of the well and run toward the ranch house, a flaming torch of dry grass wrapped around a lance. Before the Indian could throw the flames, Chisholm's .52 caliber slug ripped through his chest, pitching him backward, the burning lance falling harmlessly in front of the dead warrior.

There was a long wailing cry from the fringes of the brush nearest the barn, and Chisholm saw a burning arrow arch toward the ranch house's thatched roof. It fell short. The tall man fired three times, as quickly as he could lever the Spencer. The rounds slammed into the brush where he had spotted the archer. Chisholm rolled to his right as soon as he fired the last shot, leaving a pall of blue smoke where he had been. He heard a cry of pain from the brush.

Then there was silence.

Nothing happened for five minutes. No one moved, not a sound came except the chickens scratching in the yard.

Chisholm returned the two-foot sabre to his scabbard and locked it in place, then checked the knife on his leg and the six-shot .44 on his right hip. Satisfied, he again changed positions, edging closer to the ranch house.

The pistol fire from beyond the house came as a surprise, even though Chisholm had realized that was the blind spot. He had recognized the man as a Chiricahua Apache, and knew they could move across a plain in daylight and not be seen. They were the strongest, the cleverest, the cruelest of all the Apache tribes. As he watched, flaming arrows arched toward the house roof. Now he saw that the roof on the house was better made than the previous one he had seen. This one had more rafters, evidently because it was a sod roof with dry grass on it from the spring rains, and only gave the impression of a thatching.

The grass burned quickly, giving off a gush of smoke, but then died out revealing the thick sod. This roof would not burn through. The Indians realized it as soon as Chisolm did.

A few moments later he heard a shout

from behind him in the twisted native undergrowth.

"We will meet again, Longknife," the voice said in Spanish. "And next time your scalplock of red hair will ride my belt to my tipi."

The tall man bent to the ground as he heard the horses running. More than a dozen, he estimated. His own mount was safe. He had left the gelding south of the ranch, knowing the raiders would ride on north when they were finished here, into the mountains and the safety the rugged lands afforded them. They would take their booty from the raids, their horses and mules, and hurry back into their sanctuary, perhaps somewhere high in the Salt River Canyon.

Chisholm waited for half an hour before he moved. The hostiles would not leave a lone marksman behind to ambush him. It wasn't the way of the Apache.

He waited another few minutes, then hailed the ranch defenders.

"Hello, inside the house! It looks clear! They've gone! I'm coming out from the south! I'll have a Spencer rifle in my hands over my head! The raiders are gone! It should be safe now!"

Chisholm hated to talk that much, but it

was better than getting his head blown off by some nervous and scared rancher. These people had little enough protection out here; they had every right to be frightened. He walked into the open and, with the rifle over his head, kept a steady pace toward the back door of the adobe.

The door edged open cautiously, a rifle barrel sliding out, followed by the same man he had seen before. He was in his mid-twenties, thin, with brown hair and a long neck.

"Where in hell did you come from, mister?" the rancher asked.

"From your neighbors to the south — or what's left of them. Looks like I got here just in time."

"The Barlows?" the rancher said nodding. "They all right, ain't they?"

"None of them is hurting a bit," Chisolm said grimly. Then: "But you and I should get back over there and dig some graves right soon."

The rancher was stunned. "Dead? How many?"

"All I saw. Man and two children."

"Lord a'mighty!" The man looked up and shook his head slowly. "Probably got the woman too, or carried her off. Lord, looks like we owe you more than we can pay."

"Just a cup of coffee, friend, then we better take a shovel and get moving."

Wade Chisholm rode into the bivouacked garrison of the 5th U.S. Cavalry just before dark that evening. He was dirty, tired, and hungry. The troop was camped on the outskirts of a small town called Phoenix, some 75 miles south of the army's Department of Arizona headquarters in Prescott. He rode directly to the stable area, ignoring the challenge of the lackadaisical guard. Chisholm stripped his mount, rubbed him down, then saw that he got army rations of oats and water before he looked up at the sergeant who came up and watched him.

"Sure now, Mr. Chisholm, and the major will be wanting a word with you, the sacred moment you can tear yourself away from the welfare of that beautiful animal," the sergeant said.

Chisholm chuckled. "I hoped that I could get a rise out of you, you ugly Irishman. But I must say it's good to hear your brogue again. How long has it been, Kelly, maybe six months . . . ?"

"Four months, Chisholm, as you well remember. But when the army needs the best Indian expert in Arizona, it sends out word for Wade Chisholm to amble in for

16

duty . . . that is, if he has a mind to do it and if he can find the troop."

"Then you're looking at trouble again?"

"Aye, lad, that we are. The raiders, coming out of the mountains again, and the Colonel says he wants the problem stopped once and for all. The last ones have been Chiricahua, your old friends. You know what the army says: it takes an Apache to catch an Apache."

"Then, my low Irish friend, I can catch only half an Apache, as I'm sure you know my Indian mother would agree."

They walked through the camp, where hastily thrown bedrolls were being aligned and some semblance of order was emerging as the troop of about 200 men settled down to the overnight bivouac. They were on a patrol, so no tents or other unnecessary gear was permitted. Except for the officers. Two supply wagons were authorized and they carried food and supplies and ammunition and the officer's tents.

The two friends moved toward the Major's tent. It was white, a wall tent, set apart from the rest, the canvass pinned into the rocky soil with railroad spikes and long iron stakes. A sentry at the flap came to attention as the two walked up. Right behind them came Captain Arthur J. Thornton,

17

second in command, an officer Chisholm knew and would rather not.

"So, it has been Chisholm we've been waiting for," Thornton said. He returned the guard's salute, pushed past the two men and into the tent through the flap. Chisholm and Sergeant Kelly followed cautiously.

"Kelly, you had no permission. . . ."

"At ease, Captain." A square-set man in his forties sitting in a folding chair behind a makeshift desk of packing boxes spoke calmly, but with a slight frown of impatience at Thornton. "Thanks for bringing Mr. Chisholm in as soon as you could, Sergeant Kelly. That will be all."

Sergeant Kelly saluted, did a smart about-face, and left the tent flap after winking at Chisholm.

The scout stood, feet apart, hands on his hips, the long knife still strapped over his back. He stared without smiling at the major.

"I'm afraid I don't know you, Major, you must be new. Have you hunted the Apache on his own land before?"

"Mr. Chisholm, that is insubordinate and uncalled for," Captain Thornton rumbled.

"At ease, Captain. This is a special man you're talking to. He has the highest rating

18

in the entire Army of the West, both as an expert on Indians and as a field scout. He's had more engagements to his credit than half this patrol combined. He also gets paid more than a Captain. It's time for Mr. Chisholm and I to have a long talk. Will you excuse us, Captain? And ask the orderly to bring in that bottle of sipping whiskey I like."

The captain scowled at Chisholm, snapped a salute to the major. "Whatever the major says," he replied, turned abruptly and went through the flap.

"Is it true the Indians call you Half-Man," the major asked. "Why is that?"

Chisholm sat down in a chair at the side of the desk without waiting to be asked. He always made it a point to emphasize to newcomers that he was not army, and that he was not bound by army protocol or traditions.

"I thought you would know from my file, Major. They call me that because I'm only half Chiricahua Apache. They say I'm only half a man because I am half roundeye." He paused and sized up the army man. "I answered your question, now I'd like to know your name, Major."

"Yes, I wondered how long it would be before you asked. I like that. I think you and I are going to get along very well." He indicated a sheaf of papers in front of him held together with a large metal clip. "You have quite a record, Chisholm. Some exemplary missions. I see you were born and raised in an Apache camp and captured by us roundeyes when you were twelve. Isn't that unusual for a boy of twelve, raised as an Indian, to switch suddenly and take to white man's ideas, language, education?"

"If you know that much you should know why, too, Major. My red hair meant I was an outcast in the Indian camp. It was impossible for me to pass as an Apache. Everyone knew I was a breed. I had to be twice as strong, twice as tough, twice as mean as any of the other Indian boys my age to survive. I learned my lessons well — and I did survive. I waited for the day when I could escape from the Indian camps. So you see, my story isn't so strange after all."

"Mmmmmmmm. And in three years at a mission school, and then two more years in Omaha, you mastered as much book learning as our regular students assimilate in twelve years?"

"I had a late start, Major, and I was used to having to be twice as good as anyone else . . . to survive. It made a difference."

"Yes, yes, I can see that." The major stood

and walked to the far edge of the tent, then came back. If the man had a parade grounds he would have paced to the end of it, Chisholm was sure. "Oh, I'm Major Black, William H. Black. I'm from Virginia and my family was on the wrong side back in Sixty-one. My file in Washington reflects that fact. So I too have had to be twice as good as anyone else to get this far in the army. And the men in higher ranks have assured me that this is as high a rank as I'll ever get. So we have something in common. I'm a half-man too, half one side and half the other." He sat down and peaked his fingers, then accepted the bottle and two glasses an orderly brought in.

"Straight or with some branch water?"

"Straight."

"Yes, Chisholm, I agree."

He poured and they both sipped at the whiskey. Chisholm watched the major and liked him. Black seemed to have a lot more common sense than most of the ranking army people he had worked for and against in the field. Black had a square chin, his clean-shaven face showed the effects of many days of sun and wind on the trail. There was a relaxed confidence about the man that put Chisholm at ease. He found the idea that the major felt much the same way about him as satisfying.

"You asked how much Indian fighting I've done, Chisholm, and to be frank with you, none. This is my first command in the west, west of Chicago that is, and I'm looking forward to it. I am a commander who delegates. But I delegate only to those who are qualified to do the job, and who I have confidence in. I've been in one or another armies since I was seventeen, and before that in a military school. This is all so you can have some background about me, just as I have about you."

Chisholm drained his glass and reached for a refill.

"Major, I must admit when I saw Captain Thornton out there, I was a mite depressed. But now, after this little talk, I feel one whole lot better. It's also been some time since I've seen a friendly face in a blue coat — or had any sippin' whiskey as good as this." He lifted his refilled glass in a salute.

"Mr. Chisholm, I think we're going to work together well," Black said, raising his glass briefly, returning the salute.

"I was about to say the same thing, Major Black. Just keep Thornton out of the way." He stared into his whiskey for a moment. "Now, tell me what the hell this 'little job,' as you put it in your message, is all about."

CHAPTER 2
PURSUE AND CAPTURE

"So that's it, Mr. Chisholm. Our basic orders are to locate, pursue and capture any and all Apache raiders who have been pillaging property and murdering the residents of the Territory of Arizona. We have a free hand exactly how this is to be accomplished, but it is to be finished before the end of the year, before January 1, 1873."

"It may be a while before you hear about it, Major. So perhaps I should tell you. I stumbled onto an Indian raid earlier today. I came to two ranches that had been burned to the ground and all the people killed. The livestock was gone at each place. At the third ranch I got there in time to warn the rancher and break up the attack. I saw two of the hostiles; both were Chiricahua."

Briefly, he told the major the rest of the story about the raiders.

"And you say they headed back toward the Superstitions?"

"Yes, they were angling over that way."

"Could you find the trail again?"

"A trail of a dozen mounts? Blindfolded and hopping on one leg."

"They were heading east of Phoenix?"

"Yes, sir. I'd guess Blind Man's Canyon. That's about eighteen miles east of here."

"You said you estimated a force of twelve Apache?"

"At least. . . ."

Major Black looked at his pocket watch, then snapped the cover on it. "Three o'clock. Four more hours of good daylight left. I'll get a patrol ready to leave immediately. You'll go along as scout. Draw rations, a new mount, bedroll, anything else you need. Guard!" He called the last word loudly and the man outside stepped into the tent and, standing stiffly erect, saluted.

"Sir?"

"Send for Sergeant Kelly at once. And ask Captain Thornton to come here immediately."

The private saluted and left.

"Thornton going along on the ride?" Chisolm asked, his eyes narrowing.

Black leaned back in his chair and shrugged. "He's the most experienced man I have. I'm hoping that you two can work together. You'll have twenty enlisted men, a new second lieutenant, and Sergeant Kelly. I want you to determine the exact location where the hostiles entered the Superstitions. My reports show they usually end up there, but we don't know where they vanish to."

"Maybe they turn into spirits, Major."

"Maybe. But the U.S. Army doesn't think so." Black paused and blotted a line of perspiration from his head with a white handkerchief. "Is it always this hot here? I need a bucket of ice to sit on. Instead, I suggest we both have one more shot for the trail, Mr. Chisholm. I want you to stay while I give Captain Thornton his orders."

Five minutes later Captain Thornton stared at the major with a new appreciation.

"So, sir. We run our patrol, track the hostiles, attempt to attack and capture or kill them if possible, and, if not, trail them to the farthest reaches of their hideout and attempt to learn the location of their camps. Later we will return in force to engage the entire enemy force."

"Exactly. You will be in charge, Captain, but I suggest you rely heavily on the advice and discretion of Mr. Chisholm. He'll be your scout. He contacted this band of hostiles earlier today and has a special interest in seeing them brought to justice."

Captain Thornton snorted. "Yes sir. I

know all about Mr. Chisholm's special interests. I'll see about my men." Without another word, he saluted, turned on his heel, and exited the tent.

Chisholm looked at the major and slowly, almost sadly, shook his head.

A half hour later they were moving. Chisholm sat a new horse, but in the same army saddle he had brought in. It was hot and dry in the August afternoon. The temperature at the major's tent had read 105 degrees. The new men complained about the heat, but it was insignificant to Chisholm. He had experienced much worse heat.

There were twenty-one enlisted men, including Kelly, in addition to Captain Thornton and a young Lieutenant named Donner. This was Donner's first duty assignment out of West Point and he was glad to get the post. Most of the newly commissioned second lieutenants coming out of the academy had to wait for an opening in the officer's corps.

Every man carried rations for six days in saddle-bags, and one day's supply of water. They would get more water at the Salt River when they got there. Captain Thornton had tried to make a truce with Chisholm before they had left.

"Look, Chisholm. I know we've never really gotten along in the past, but we both have jobs to do now. Let's get the work done, then we can get out of each other's sight."

Chisholm had grinned at the captain, shot a wad of tobacco juice an inch from his polished boot, and nodded.

"I don't look for trouble, Captain. I'll do my job, you don't have to worry about that. But I'll expect you to rely on my judgment and my recommendations when it comes to the Apache."

"If it's a military matter. . . ."

Chisholm had cut him off so short that the Captain had taken a step backward.

"Military? For God's sakes, Thornton, don't you ever read the records on your people? I had captain's bars on my shoulder when you were still in officer's school. I figured you damn well knew that by now."

"I thought you would want everyone to forget that. You were a toy, a two-star general's toy. You used that old man."

Chisholm had lunged toward Thornton, but stopped himself just before he swung his fist. He had spun away, checked out his new mount, and lifted into the saddle. He would speak to the captain only when ordered to do so. Let him find his own God-damned Apache trail.

An hour later, Thornton had them angling across the low, hot desert east of Phoenix on an intercept course with the trail that should be heading toward Blind Man's Canyon. Chisholm had let the captain lead the way, content to bring up the tail end of the line of horses, swallowing trail dust, but at least alone with his thoughts.

He had no idea why he had let his emotions surge up in him back at the bivouac. The lie was nothing he hadn't heard before, dozens, hundreds of times, and eventually it had been the reason he resigned his commission and went into scouting. At least he could be around the army, near the military, without having to suffer because of it. But it had come back, once again.

The captain's orderly, a young corporal, rode down the line of march and waved at Chisholm. Dust caked thin sweat lines on the corporal's face.

"Mr. Chisholm. The captain requests your presence at the head of the column."

"Yeah. Right. I'll be along. You ride on back."

When the corporal had left, Chisholm pushed his way out of the line of march dust and rode to the head of the column.

"Nice of you to join us, Mr. Chisholm,"

Thornton said.

"Wondered when you were going to ask, Captain."

"Scout ahead and see if you can pick up the hostile's trail. We've got an hour before dusk. I want to nail down the trail before dark if we can, then move up to the canyon on a night ride."

Chisholm nodded, swung his horse away from the column and angled toward the Superstition Mountains in the distance. He was back on the desert. He remembered how everyone in Chicago thought that a desert was a dead place. It was dry, hot, empty, without a self-respecting tree for twenty miles. But it wasn't dead. There was life here, a whole chain of life if you knew how to find it. Chisholm knew. The Apache knew.

He had ridden less than half an hour when he spotted it. Chisholm got off his mount and checked for sure: tracks of more than twenty horses and mules, some shod some not. Five of the mounts pushed prints deeper into the sand showing that they had either riders or were pack animals. The party had passed there about six hours before.

Chisholm ground-tied his mount, gathered some dry cactus, and built a small fire, then broke off green branches from some chaparral and piled them on the fire to make a column of blue-gray smoke. He sat down against a rock and pulled his black, high-crowned hat down over his eyes.

Fifteen minutes later the patrol arrived at the burned out fire. Chisholm had seen them heading his way and let the brim of his hat fall back over his eyes. He waited until Captain Thornton nudged him with his boot.

"Chisholm, you found the trail?"

"That's what the army pays me to do, Captain. You're standing on the hoofprints. They changed directions. Looks like they're moving closer to Salt Creek. I'd say the second canyon over from where I first thought. One canyon west of the stream."

"Then let's ride. We'll get as close to the mountains as we can tonight, camp, and move out first thing in the morning."

"There's no hurry, Captain. The Apaches passed here six hours ago. That means they're into the mountains, have their guards out. And they're probably drinking and feasting to celebrate the prizes they've brought back. Unless we're lucky, we won't see hide nor toenail of those Apaches, nor the horses they stole."

"But we will try, Mr. Chisholm," Thornton said firmly. "I expect your tracking work will only just begin after we get into the mountains."

They rode until dark, then stopped for cold field rations of salt pork and hardtack. Each man had ten pounds on his back and it was supposed to last him five days. There would be no hot grub that night — all in the best cavalry tradition.

The sun was down now but it was still hot. Sergeant Kelly estimated it was still at least 95 degrees. It would cool down little more during the night. The men grumbled, took care of their mounts, let them rest for two hours, then it was boots and saddles again as they mounted and, two abreast, moved out across the desert in the dim moonlight. The last man in the line of march led a small remuda of three army horses, two with small packs, and a third with a saddle. They were spare mounts in case some of the other horses were hurt or killed.

They rode until just before ten p.m. when Captain Thornton called a halt. The patrol had arrived at the Salt River and there was enough fresh water in it to take care of both the horses and the men.

Ever since darkness fell there had been little real tracking. Every mile or so Chisholm had put a lighted lantern to the ground and tried to pick up the tracks. Sometimes he found them, but more often he didn't. Now he relaxed a moment by the river. It came out of its gorge here and flowed peacefully along the low lying desert.

Chisholm got up and watered his horse at the stream, then pulled off the saddle and blanket and rubbed down the bay. She was a strong horse, and he wanted her to stay that way. A cavalry man's first allegiance is to his horse on the trail. Without that horse he is walking and, in Indian country, especially in the Arizona desert in August, it could be his last walk.

When his mount was taken care of, Chisholm spread out his blankets and stared up at the stars. A moment later a runner found him and said Captain Thornton had requested his presence.

"Figures," Chisholm said walking back with the private. "How old are you?" he asked.

"Eighteen, sir."

"I'm not a sir. Why did you sign on?"

"To get a job. To earn some money. And to get out of Boston."

"Son, you are really out of Boston."

Captain Thornton and Donner were fifty feet from the others on a slight rise so they could see the dark lumps of the men spread out below them. The officers had a lantern lit and were looking at maps.

Chisholm scowled at the lantern. "If this were hostile country both of you would be dead by now," he said.

"This isn't hostile country, Mr. Chisholm," Thornton said evenly. "What do you know about the Superstition Mountains?"

"I was born and raised in them, as you should know, Captain."

"What part of them?"

"All of them. I didn't have a permanent house number. My tribe moved around a lot to get away from murdering roundeyes."

Donner grinned but didn't let Thornton see it.

"Mr. Chisholm," the captain began with a deep sigh, "I'm not interested in your wit, your humor or any insubordination from you. You're a scout and a tracker, and I want you to confine yourself to those duties. Can you track this band once it gets into the mountains?"

"Yes, up to a point. When they get on the bare rock trails I'll lose them. It depends on how far you want to penetrate, how much time you give me to raise the trail again when they ride off the slabs of rock."

"That's about what our last scout said. I

thought you were better."

Chisholm felt his anger rising, and turned away for a few steps, then came back. "Thornton, you are not a stupid man. Why are you talking this way, simply to get me angry? Remember, if you get me all fired up on the trail I could make a mistake, and that would please you greatly. However, if I make a big enough mistake you and every trooper here would die right alongside me. Just remember that as your hatred for me boils."

"Lieutenant Donner, you're excused. This is something Chisholm and I need to talk about privately."

"Yes sir," Donner said. "I'll see you in the morning." He walked into the night.

When Thornton turned into the glow of the lantern, Chisholm saw that his face was purple with fury. He balled his fists and used a lot of control to hold down his temper.

"Mr. Chisholm. I didn't ask for this patrol. I didn't want to come if you were the scout. But how dare you insult me in front of a subordinate. You did it deliberately. You're army enough to know how that undermines an officer's authority, his command. If you ever do anything like that again, I'll see that you return to camp tied across the back of a horse, dead or alive it won't matter to me."

"Art, that sounds just like you," Chisholm drawled. "I just sincerely hope that wasn't meant to be a threat. The last man who threatened to kill me is now pushing up clover in a meadow in Flagstaff. Now that you've had your big thrill of the day, I suggest we work out some perimeters for this patrol. Just how far do you want to penetrate? Do you know where any of the summer or winter camps are the Apache use in the Superstitions? Exactly how big a risk factor do you want to sign for on this patrol action?"

Thornton took a step backward. He wasn't used to having men stand up to him, to answer a threat with a threat, and it shocked and angered him. He slowly regained his composure, but his eyes continued to glare with sparks of hatred.

"Chisholm, I've no intention of putting up with you. I'm sending a rider back to Phoenix at daylight to bring in another scout."

"You don't have another scout," Chisholm said, taking a step nearer Thornton. "You're not at Prescott now, you're in the field. You still panic under pressure, don't you? Just like at Swallow River Camp. I'm stuck with you and you're saddled with me.

I just hope to God that you don't get us all killed."

"You can't talk that way to me," Thorton barked, stiffening.

"Why not? Your witness isn't here. And you don't have guts enough to fight it out with bayonets. So settle down, get a grip on your nerves, and let's work out the patrol. How far do you want to follow them? How big a risk do you want to take? Every mile we forge into the mountains means we have four times as much risk. Five miles in will make it twenty times harder to get out than one mile in. Do you like those odds? That's why the hostiles are safe in there. To root them out you're going to have to get some inside information, then get a company-sized force at least. And even then you'll be damn lucky to get out of it with your scalp." Chisholm heaved a deep breath. "Look, first you have to find out exactly where they're camped and why the spot gives them such tremendous protection."

Thornton stared at him for a minute without speaking. Twice he started, then stopped. At last: "You really are a bastard, aren't you, Chisholm. You bait me just enough to open old wounds, to get me boiling mad but not enough to reach the explosion point. And everyone knows that you have high ranking friends at headquarters in Prescott. So I'll play your little game and hope to God that you don't get us all killed, especially me."

He pointed to the map. "We are situated here, just outside the Salt Creek gorge. We have twenty men and we are not designed to be an attack force to wipe out the entire Apache nation. We are concerned with one raiding party that attacked several ranches. If we can't find them with a reasonable effort, we break off the mission and return to our bivouac."

"Fine, now just what is a reasonable effort?"

"We'll follow the tracks as far as we can, protecting ourselves from attack at all times. We will not proceed so far into the mountains that we might be cut off. This patrol will serve more than one end. We now have four separate probes such as this one on record, and by coordinating the trails the hostiles take, it could give us some indication where they are hiding, and how they vanish so quickly."

"Sounds reasonable. But remember, the Apache doesn't live by the rules, he makes his own. And never think you can surprise them, especially the Chiracahua. You won't."

"We won't even try, mister. We'll follow

37

the usual trail schedule for tomorrow. Now we both better get some sleep while we can. It's hard telling when we'll get any more. Any questions?"

"Nope, not a one. I just hope your bugler has a good alarm clock."

He did. They moved out promptly at six the next morning.

CHAPTER 3
FIRE AND MOVE

The troop rode at six a.m. but Chisholm had been up and moving since first light, working the area in front of the canyon mouth, then moving to the east for three miles. He found the trail of the raiders a mile south of the river. They had not gone into the Salt River gorge directly. Rather, they had gone up a small ravine, then wound over a pair of low ridges before dropping down into the gorge. Then they had worked upstream in the shallows for half a mile before coming out on the opposite bank and following a well-worn trail along the water upstream.

Chisholm rode out to the mouth of the canyon just as the troop had assembled for inspection. He went directly to Thornton and made his report.

Thornton was interested but not impressed. "We knew they were going into the gorge, Chisholm. What difference does it make how they got there? We'll proceed into the canyon and you can pick up the trail where you left it."

An hour later, Chisholm moved cautiously up the trail along the Salt River. He doubted if there were any lookouts this far downstream. The trail was clear where the band of horses and mules had been driven up the trail. Here and there the herd crossed sheets of rock and there were no prints to find, but on the other side Chisholm picked up the trail again.

A quarter of a mile farther along they came to an area of crumbled shale that made footing uncertain and wiped out all sign of any tracks. The shale was a long stretch of over half a mile, with numerous small side arroyos and canyons that angled away from the Salt River. Chisholm ignored them and pressed on, anxious to be through with the shale. He had been through this section of the gorge many times as a boy, and he remembered most of it, but not all. The winter rains and flash floods had changed the details but not the general structure.

Thornton was getting more nervous with each quarter mile. Twice in an hour he had dispatched his orderly up to Chisholm for a report; each time the scout told the captain to wait. If the tracks were on the other side of the shale they would continue. If they were not, a decision would need to be made.

Chisholm could see the captain's reaction: the tightening of Thornton's neck muscles, his narrowed eyes darting about in fear. Chisholm felt there was no real danger, not yet anyway. The Apaches weren't going to give themselves away by an attack on a small force, unless it could guarantee that there would be no survivors. That would take planning, including an advance party to cut off any retreat. The Apaches were not that well organized in warfare. Planning had always been their weak point. Marvelous as individual fighters, they quickly fell apart when structured into a military force that needed to act on orders and in coordination; it was this flaw that Chisholm knew would one day mean their ultimate destruction.

The scout was walking now, leading his mount, studying the ground in front of him. They were at last across the shale but now, after two hundred yards, there was only a narrow ledge beside the stream — and it had not been traveled by a horse in several weeks. The walls of the gorge at this point were well over a hundred feet high, not straight up, but still too steep for a horse.

41

He signalled a halt and returned to where the captain sat on his horse in the middle of the column, a cocked pistol in his right hand.

He had lost the trail, Chisholm was sure of it now. Somewhere along the half mile of shale the hostiles had turned off. But where . . . ? There were half a dozen gullies branching off from the gorge, none of them very deep, but which one did the Indians use?

"You've lost the trail, haven't you," Thornton said before Chisholm could speak.

"Yes, they turned off. Now it's a matter of working out each of these small canyons intersecting the trail until we find the right one."

The captain sent word to dismount. The men would rest the horses while Chisholm scoured the canyons for Indian signs.

"I'd like to take Sergeant Kelly with me," Chisholm said. "He understands these mountains — and the Apache."

"Granted." Thornton paused. "Chisholm, it's said you can sense the Apache when he's around. Are we being watched right now? Does the Apache band know we're chasing them?"

"They know. They expect to be followed after every raid, and so they take precautions. Watching us now? I doubt it. If I were in a secure position, I'd have only two lookouts, but close to my main camp. We may be twenty miles from where the hostiles are bedded down. No, I don't think any of them are watching us. I don't feel their eyes on the back of my neck."

"I can feel them, Chisholm," Thornton said, glancing quickly at the canyon walls.

"Relax, Captain. No one is interested in us yet. Remember this isn't like it was at Swallow River Camp."

Thornton stiffened, then, without a word, turned and rode to the water and allowed his mount to drink.

Chisholm's eyes burned into Thornton's blue-coated back, then he, too, turned away. He couldn't let the chance pass; he had to mention Swallow River Camp to see Thornton's reaction.

Kelly laughed when Chisholm found him near the end of the line of march and called him out. "I need somebody I can trust, Kelly, and you're it. We need to take a hike. Got any bounce left in those Irish legs of yours?"

"More than you'd want to know about, lad. They be for going up one of these shale gullies, I'd wager."

"Aye, that we will be, laddie," Chisholm said, dropping into the heavy Irish brogue.

"And it's up to us to do it now."

They left their horses, but took their rifles as they worked the farthest gully, the last one before they saw that they had lost the prints. It was a slow trip, pawing and scratching to the top. The shale footing was impossible. In places for each step forward, they slid half a step backward. At last they found a solid shelf, and worked that another hundred yards to the summit of the ravine. The shale ended, but on the top of the ridge there were no hoofprints in the soft sand and dirt. The hostiles had not come up that way.

"What now?" Chisholm asked Kelly as a test.

The Irishman chuckled. "So we're still in school, are we? What I say is that sure and it's past time for a pull at that jug of good Irish whiskey, if that's what you still carry in that canteen of yours."

Chisholm passed his canteen to the other man who opened it and sniffed, laughed and took a short-pull.

"I'll not be runnin' you short, lad. Since I have a private stock in me saddlebags." He looked up. "We go over this connecting ridge and down the next ravine?"

"We could. Instead let's work the tops of the four gullies until we find the tracks we

44

need, if they are here."

They worked slowly along the razorback, watching closely for sign of hoofprints, or massive amounts of disturbed shale. They found neither.

It was an hour later when they hiked back up to where the patrol waited. Wearily, Chisholm reported to Thornton.

"Nothing. That means they didn't go up those trails. It probably means that they did cross the river and worked up the other side in some way." Chisholm took a chew on a chunk of beef jerky from his pocket, and watched the patrol's commander.

"How much more time do you need to check that out?"

"To find their trail, maybe half a day. Unless you want to say that we have made a reasonable effort and want to head back."

Thornton hesitated and, in doing so, gave Chisholm a moment to laugh quietly.

The captain's jaw snapped shut forming a grim line. "Find the trail. We'll stay here the night if we need to. We'll be in that wide spot down a quarter of a mile. I'll have out plenty of security, so don't worry, Mr. Chisholm. We'll all be here when you get back."

Sergeant Kelly and Chisholm found a shallow place and forded the river on foot, holding their rifles high over their heads. They got to the far bank, checked the narrow slope of land, then moved upstream. They checked out the first ravine but found nothing. On the third one, less than ten feet out of the water, they found the first print of an unshoed horse, then another, and soon the pattern was established.

Kelly grinned. "You're right, lad. Less than a day old and heading upstream. But in this little ravine they can't go a half mile."

"Let's find out how far they do go," Chisholm said. The ravine was less than a quarter of a mile long, narrow, barren and hot. The tracks kept moving up the center of it past the midway point, then they angled to one side and moved at an angle along the side of the ravine. Soon they were at the top of the small ridge. Quickly they went forward and up another ridge, then straight across a wider valley with a smattering of green and some few trees to another ridge, again turning right into the interior of the Superstition Mountains.

Now they were two ridges over from the main gorge. The tracks kept moving upstream, climbing gradually, not staying long in the bottom land, but moving to another ridge. The next small valley came and with it a few more trees, where the rainfall had gathered and collected to give life to a few small trees.

Chisholm called a halt and they sat under the shade of the trees as the scout looked at the sun. "Time we headed back," Chisholm said.

"I'll look forward to fording that river again," Kelly said. "Cool me off. What about tomorrow?"

"It's up to Thornton. Whatever he says. We need a larger force, even for a probe like this. We have a better direction than I've known about before. Perhaps we're closer to their camp than we realize. But we need more guns, more protection, and a much larger force if it's to be a strike."

They retraced their steps, knowing the way now, making better time than on the way up. They were two hundred yards from the main gorge when they heard rifle fire.

Both men broke into a run toward the last ridge where they could look down on the troops. By the time they got there the pony soldiers were pinned down.

Both men saw the situation at once. On the far side of the river on the ridge, two parties of Apaches were firing down into the troops.

Kelly pointed to the group on his right. Chisholm took those on the left and aimed his big .52 caliber Spencer repeater.

"Tell me when you're ready, Kelly. We'll let go at the same time."

Kelly said, "Now," and they both fired. They each sent seven rounds into the Apache's positions, then slid back away from the ridgeline for protection as they reloaded. They ran ten yards down the ridge, took one incoming round that missed, then found new firing positions. Half the hostiles had abandoned their positions. Chisholm and Kelly were above the enemy and had an advantage. Again the two men fired their seven rounds, aiming carefully and dropping two more of the Apaches before the last of them melted back into the downslope and vanished.

By the time Chisholm and Kelly got down to the river and waded across, order had been restored. Lt. Donner stood over Thornton, agitation and worry clouding his face. He turned as Kelly came up.

"Sergeant, make a count, see how many dead and wounded we have. Then prepare for a night march. We're getting out of this trap just as soon as it's dark."

Chisholm looked at Thornton. The man's eyes were wild, his hands tied at his sides, and then Chisholm saw that the captain's feet had also been tied together. There was a rough bandage around his right thigh and another one on his left shoulder.

"Mr. Chisholm, we've had a bit of a problem here," Donner said. "I had to take command. The captain was wounded and not fit to be in charge."

"I understand, Lieutenant. Just be sure you make a thorough and complete report to Major Black as soon as we return. Have witnesses, as many of the men as you can get. Order them to write down their observations of how the captain acted — and make sure they sign the statements."

"Yes, sir. I certainly will."

"Without witnesses your testimony won't mean a thing. In fact it could put you in a serious position where you might even be charged."

"But he was out of his mind! He jumped up and ran away. He hid behind his horse, then was hit and began screaming, tearing out his hair. I've never seen such a demonstration of cowardice under fire before by any man."

"Make certain to get your witnesses, or it will turn out just like last time at Swallow River Camp," Chisholm said.

They began the march out as soon as it was dark, and it took them almost to midnight to clear the canyons. Then they camped near where they had been before on the desert beside the Salt River. Lieutenant Donner had given the men his instructions and told them to keep the incident plainly in their minds, but not to talk about it. As soon as writing equipment was available in the morning, each man would be asked to write down or dictate what he saw happen concerning Captain Thornton.

The captain had been tied to his saddle for the first few hours, his feet bound together under the mount's belly. But by the time they reached the desert floor, he had lost his fright and settled into an angry surly mood. He would talk to no one.

By first call at six o'clock, Thornton bounced out of his blankets, back to normal. He winced at his wounds, stared at them for a moment, then evidently chose to ignore them. Donner had been talking with Kelly and Chisholm as they watched the captain get out of his blankets and yell for his orderly the way he usually did.

"He's back to normal. What the hell do I do now?" Donner asked.

"You do exactly what the captain tells you," Kelly said. "When we get back to the bivouac area, you, me and Mr. Chisholm will have a long talk with the major. Just hang tight and don't let him get to you."

"Kelly's right, Donner," Chrisholm said. "Otherwise he could have you up on a whole passel of charges before you know what hit you."

"I'll wait, you can bet on that. But I've got three dead troopers tied over their mounts and he doesn't even recognize the fact or notice his own wounds. I wonder if he remembers anything about last night?"

"Probably nothing," Chisholm said. "Isn't this the captain's orderly coming up?"

"Yeah," Kelly said. "We're being summoned."

The corporal ran up to them, stopped and looked at the civilian. "Mr. Chisholm, you're wanted at the captain's quarters. He said immediately."

"All right, son. You run along. I'll be there."

When the corporal was out of hearing, Chisholm grumbled at the other two men, then motioned for Donner to follow. Both men took long strides toward where Thornton stood beside his bedroll. They had had to force him into his blankets the previous night over his wild protests. Now he smiled at the scout and his junior officer.

"Well, Chisholm, Donner, good to see you. Chisholm, you got in last night after we made our move. What is your evaluation of the enemy stronghold?"

"I didn't find the stronghold. But the mission is complete, Captain. Sergeant Kelly and I penetrated to a new ridgeline, but the trail failed to indicate any practical information about the eventual destination of the hostiles. I'll have a complete report for you as soon as we get back to the bivouac area."

"Bivouac? Are we ready to go back?" Thornton blinked, obviously perplexed.

"You said last night that our mission was complete, sir," Chisholm replied matter-of-factly. "And that we would march out to this position in the dark to avoid any hostiles, then be ready for a quick ride back to the rest of the force so we could report to Major Black."

"Yes, of course," Thornton said, nodding his head as though he remembered issuing the orders. "I just thought that by now you might have remembered some new data that might alter those plans. You spoke of going at the enemy from another known entry port."

"I don't see the value of it now, Captain. No, I think you were right in ordering the march back this morning. Well, it is almost time for boots and saddles. I better get my gear cleaned and packed. With your permission, sir . . . ?"

"What? Oh, yes, Sergeant Chisholm, you must be ready to ride. You're dismissed, Sergeant."

Grinning, Chisholm did a snappy salute, an about-face, and walked away with Donner.

"I don't believe what I just heard," the young Lieutenant said. "You convinced him that *he* gave the order to pull out and that *he* ordered the march back to the bivouac. Amazing. And he thought you were a sergeant."

"His mind is still playing tricks on him, but he's trying with all of his might to maintain control, maintain the status quo, to hold together. He's tough, Donner. In a month he won't believe a word you said about his condition. He will fight you to the last breath. Which is what he did once before — and even got promoted afterwards."

"May the good Lord help us all," Donner said. They walked back to the spot they had been. Donner's boyish face suddenly seemed older, more experienced. "Thanks, Chisholm. I appreciate what you did back there. You probably saved my military career."

"Think nothing of it, you can use mine.

And you're damn right you appreciate it, Lieutenant. When we get back to camp I'll help you form up your charges, then you get your ass busy getting the enlisted men to write those statements about the captain. I'll be the one to appreciate that!"

CHAPTER 4
THORNTON'S ORDEAL

The patrol column arrived back at the bivouac area in the early afternoon, and the idle troops quickly gathered to stare at the wounded and the three silent bodies tied over their mounts. Wild tales began at once. Chisholm hurried to the major's tent to get in the first salvo. He had briefly described the situation before Thornton came into the tent and saluted.

"Captain Thornton reporting the conclusion of a most successful patrol, sir!"

"Good, Captain, I was just getting Chisholm's estimate on the location of the hostile hideouts. How did it go?"

"I'm sure Chisholm has told you, sir. Overall, I'd say we made excellent progress in finding the location of the hostiles."

"But what about the cost, Captain. Was it worth it?" Black watched his senior officer closely.

Thornton held his wide-brimmed campaign hat in his hands, slowly turning it around and around. He seemed to look beyond Black, not at him. "The cost, sir? I don't understand."

"Yes, the cost. Your dead and wounded . . . your own wounds."

"I wasn't aware of the costs. . . . We did an outstanding job, Colonel, sir. I'm proud of my men. I'd like to put in for several decorations if it's all right with the colonel."

"Yes, Thornton, we'll talk about it later. I'll want to hear a complete report. Why don't you tell my orderly to get you a drink from my special sippin' whiskey. I'll be through with Chisholm here in a moment, then we'll have to talk."

Thornton brightened. "Thank you, sir. Yes, I understand. I could use a good drink." He snapped to attention, saluted, and marched out of the tent.

Major Black frowned. "He doesn't even recognize the fact that he has three dead and seven wounded and that he took two bullets himself. And he kept calling me colonel. He's a sick man, Chisholm. I'd like to transfer him back to Prescott at once, but you know the army. There will have to be charges filed before I can move."

"Yes, sir. Lieutenant Donner was the officer in charge. He'll file charges. I'm sure he's working on them now. Sergeant Kelly and I got back after most of it was over."

"Tell Donner to file the papers quickly. I've never seen anything quite like this before. You say he did much the same thing at the Swallow River Camp massacre, but he was never charged or relieved?"

"Yes, sir. We lost half of our patrol. A sergeant brought the troops out, the other officer was killed. Thornton snapped out of his confusion so quickly that time that no one would believe my charges. None of the enlisted men would back me up. Without an officer's testimony, they knew the charges wouldn't stick. This time I hope it will be different."

Black stood and lit his pipe. He walked to a screened window and stared out for a moment, then returned to the desk and sat down. "Chisholm, you realize he is an officer, and a lower ranks is charging him. You know the officer corps, how we stick together. I'll have to follow normal procedures, which means I can't do a damn thing until I get Donner's charges. Then I'll hold a preliminary hearing, and only then can I do anything about taking Thornton out of command and off the duty roster."

"Yes, sir. I appreciate that. Just don't put him in command of any more patrols, leastways nowhere that men can get killed. That should be a factor at your discretion. I don't think you want a whole patrol wiped out. They could have been yesterday if Donner had not taken firm control quickly. He did a good job."

"Yes, Chisholm, I can do that much. And I appreciate your quandry. Tell Lieutenant Donner to rush those papers. If he gets them done today it will help. I'll also need a written report from you, a scout report, nothing about the captain. You might want to write that in a separate paper if you like."

Chisholm nodded and stepped out of the tent. He saw Thornton talking with two other officers in the command, relating some wild story about how he was wounded. Chisholm was sure Thornton didn't remember a thing about it. The good old army and its officers never changed.

He borrowed some paper from the supply corporal, sat on his bedroll and wrote his scout's report. It was factual, telling exactly where the troop went, what he and Kelly did, what they found, and the general direction he figured the hostiles were heading. He said he had no idea why they were on the ridges instead of going up the Salt Creek gorge.

Chisholm completed his report with these words:

"It is therefore my opinion that a patrol of troopers will never be able to locate the hiding places of the Apaches in the Superstition Mountains. There are hundreds of hiding spots and places to ambush troops, and the Apache know them all. I would suggest that a one man scouting expedition might be much more productive than the traditional twenty man patrol, and that I should be the one to make the trip. If such a venture is approved, I will go in not as scout or trooper, but disguised as an Apache.

"I estimate that my trip into the Superstitions will take no more than a week's time, and with the information so received, it should be possible for a strong force to enter the Superstition Mountains knowing exactly where it is going, how many hostiles it would be confronting, and that such an action would meet with military success."

He read it over twice, signed it, then carried it to the major's orderly who promised that it would be in the commanding officer's hands just as soon as his current visitor left.

"Is it Captain Thornton?" Chisholm asked.

"Can't say," the orderly said, and grinned. "If'n I could, I'd sure as hell say you made a damned good guess."

Chisholm found the beef jerky in his pocket, bit off a chunk and began working on it. As he chewed, he found a small spot of shade behind the mess tent and promptly curled up and went to sleep. He had some catching up to do.

The hearing took place in Major Black's tent two days later. It was a cloudy day and it looked like an August thunderstorm was coming. Ominous strato-cumulous clouds were billowing around the rim of mountains, and the wind had freshened considerably.

There were four folding chairs in the ten-foot square command tent. Two in front. In one sat Captain Thornton. Major Black sat behind his improvised desk. Wade Chisholm held down one more chair and in the other sat Lieutenant Donner. Major Black looked up.

"It's the appointed hour, so we shall begin. Let me remind everyone that this is not a trial, nor is it a matter of record. There will be a report prepared by myself after the hearing and that will be the total official record." He turned to Thornton.

"Captain Arthur J. Thornton, you have been served with a list of charges. In addition, you have been granted twenty-four hours to study them, obtain counsel, and prepare your reply. You have informed me that you do not require counsel. Therefore, Captain, are you ready to proceed?"

Thornton glanced helplessly at Chisholm and Donner before turning to Black. "Major Black, sir," he began weakly, "this really is . . . sir, this is all nonsense. I have done nothing. . . ." He caught the stern stare from his superior and backed down. "Yes . . . sir . . . I am ready to . . . to respond. . . ."

Black nodded. "Good. Now in hearings such as this the presiding officer has wide latitude as to the methods to be used. In this case, we will read the charges and the captain will immediately have opportunity to contest, challenge, or disprove such charges."

Black paused to sip water from a glass, then looked at the papers on his desk. He picked one up. Donner coughed nervously and even Chisholm reflected the uncomfortableness in the tent by squirming in his chair.

"The charges," Black began, "that on or about August 14, 1872, while leading a unit of the 5th U.S. Cavalry on a patrol into the Superstition Mountains in the Territory of Arizona, that Captain Arthur J. Thornton did act in such a manner that he was deemed to be unable to continue commanding and was relieved of such command. To wit:

"He became extremely agitated and fell into panic when the patrol was ambushed from the cliffs above by hostiles. He screamed, held his head, then ran into exposed positions where he was felled by rifle fire from the hostiles. . . .

"After being wounded he ran for his horse and attempted to ride the animal from the scene of the battle. While in this act of deserting his command he was shot again by hostiles and fell to the ground cowering, whimpering, screaming for mercy. . . ."

Thornton moaned heavily, a man in deep emotional pain. Chisholm and Donner regarded the crestfallen man, and Donner quickly averted his eyes, unable to stomach the undignified, unmilitary sight. Major Black had paused in his reading to direct a baleful stare at Thornton. The captain cringed noticeably.

"He had to be restrained," continued Black, as he once again read from the paper, "bound hand and foot, and physically restrained under cover so he would not be shot again. . . .

"Second Lieutenant Josh Donner, acting

in accordance with military law, was forced to relieve Captain Thornton of command for the safety and well-being of his men. . . .

"Captain Thornton was unable to exercise prudent command of his officers or men, abandoning his rightful authority, and opening the twenty-two officers and men in his command to deadly peril. Three troopers on the patrol were killed by enemy action and seven wounded."

Major Black looked up and saw the shock register on Thornton's ashened face. "Captain, you may now respond to the charges."

The three men watched as Thornton slowly pulled himself to his feet, as though in a daze. Then, suddenly, he seemed to come alive. He crisply saluted Major Black, who returned the salute. Then Thornton stepped into a stiff parade rest position with his hands clasped behind his back. He looked hatefully at Chisholm for a moment, then addressed Black.

"Major. This entire document is one scandalous collection of lies, untruths, and manufactured slanders perpetrated by the only civilian present. At no time did I relinquish control of my command on the indicated patrol. At no time did I scream, shout, or attempt to flee the scene of battle. The conflict was a minor skirmish in which

I was wounded as I attempted to defend the three enlisted men who were unfortunately mortally wounded in the cowardly ambush by the Apaches."

Donner's jaw had dropped in disbelief. He glanced at Chisholm, but the scout's impassive expression was fixed on Thornton.

Angrily, Thornton swung around and thrust an accusing finger at Chisholm. "Lies — all of it lies!" he hissed, spittle collecting at the corners of his mouth. "And it all comes from a half man: a half-white, half-Apache who deserted the army and has thrown in with his savage ancestors to discredit the army. The Apache breed should be run out of this command! Lies!"

He glared at Chisholm for a long moment, then sat down.

"Lieutenant Donner, do you have proof of your charges?" Major Black asked.

Donner stood at attention, but did not salute; it was not the custom to salute in such instances.

"Yes, sir. I have proof. First is my own eye-witness testimony. I was a witness present at each of the specified acts. I was there when the first shots were fired into our patrol, which was at ease, waiting the return of our scout and Sergeant Kelly. I witnessed the entire chain of events that led to the necessity to tie the captain hand and foot and roll him into the protection of some rocks so he would not run into the open and be cut down by more enemy bullets."

"Yes, Lieutenant, I understand you have this testimony. And it has been written, submitted and duly noted. What other testimony do you have?"

"In this sheaf I have the written, sworn statements of thirteen of the living seventeen troopers who were on the patrol. The other four cannot read or write. These thirteen troopers are prepared to come and testify in person as to the activities and behavior of Captain Thornton on the afternoon in question."

"May I have the documents, please," the major said.

Donner took them to the desk.

"Any more witnesses, Lieutenant?"

"Yes, sir. That of First Sergeant Timothy Kelly, of this command. He was the highest ranking non-commissioned officer at the scene. He arrived after he had helped drive off the attackers."

"Do you have his written testimony as well?"

"I do, sir. Also I might add Scout Wade

Chisholm arrived at the same time as Sergeant Kelly, and his testimony also is included."

"Could we hear from Mr. Chisholm?" the Major asked.

The scout stood, stared at Thornton, then looked back at the major.

"What did you find when you returned from the patrol, Mr. Chisholm?" Black asked.

"The captain was tied hand and foot, lodged behind some boulders out of the line of fire from the cliff. He had been shot with minor wounds in the arm and leg to which dressings had been applied. He was not rational, would not speak with me or anyone else. He glared, shouted, made unintelligible sounds, and occasionally he let out a terrible scream."

Thornton shot to his feet. "Sir, I must protest these lies, this vicious slander! This half-breed is *not* a fellow officer! He is *not* quali—"

"Captain," Black cut in, his voice low and commanding, "you will take your seat immediately — without another word! You will have your opportunity to respond to Mr. Chisholm's testimony."

"But, sir!" Thornton protested.

"Sit, Captain! Now!"

Thornton sighed and sagged down onto his chair, his head down, his hands clenching and unclenching in total frustration.

Black looked at Chisholm. "Mr. Chisholm, you may continue. . . ."

Chisholm nodded at Black. "Yes, sir. We kept under cover till darkness, then the major was sat on his horse, tied on with hands to the pommel and his feet tied around the horse's belly. Then his mount was led out of the canyon as the troop, under the command of Lieutenant Donner, moved out of danger.

"The following morning the major seemed recovered, but he did not seem to realize that there had been a fight with the hostiles, or that there had been any losses. He made no acknowledgement of his own wounds."

Chisholm indicated he was through and the major waved him back to his seat. Black looked at Thorton. "Does the accused have any further response to the charges?"

Thornton stood slowly, then reached for the .45 that usually hung from his hip. It was not there. His eyes widened in fright, then he screamed and stormed out of the tent, slashing through the flap.

Outside there was a scuffle those in the tent could hear.

"Let me go! Let me go!" Thornton's voice

could be heard. Then the sound died away and was replaced with sobbing.

None of the men in the tent had moved. The major rapped his knuckles in the packing box.

"It is the finding of this hearing that there is sufficient cause to hold the accused and that a general courts-martial, or subsequent fitness hearings, shall be conducted by the next higher chain of command, namely the Department of Arizona Army Headquarters, in Prescott. The accused is to be transported at the first opportunity, and is hereby relieved of all his duties in this command."

Outside the tent a few moments later, Chisholm shook hands with Donner.

"Thanks. For three years I've been afraid something like this might happen again. I'm glad you were there to rally the patrol and prevent another massacre."

Donner nodded grimly and they went their separate ways.

The next day Chisholm got the go ahead for his one-man probe into the Superstitions. The first thing he did was hunt up the company barber, but the man didn't have what Chisholm wanted. Chisholm decided he would have to make it on his own.

Back at his bedroll he dug into his goods and found the buckskin leggings. He put them on, discarding his tan shirt and the army issue blue pants. He went into the brush next to the Salt River and found what he needed: the berries of the Squaw bush, and those from two other types of chaparral. Back at the camp he took his mess kit cup and mashed the berries and blended them together. Then he mashed them again and let the resulting darkening juice sit in the sun for three hours.

Next he diluted it by half with water, mixed it well, then boiled it over a small campfire for fifteen minutes. When the mixture had cooled he drained out the liquid, straining out all the seeds and pulp. He was ready.

At the river he washed his hair until it was clean, then took the pail of berry juice and slowly, carefully rinsed his hair with it. The polished steel mirror set on the bank of the river showed him his progress and, after half an hour, his bright red hair was a deep brownish black. It wasn't as long as that of most of the Apache, but it would do. He rubbed some of the berry stain into his chest and shoulders to deepen the color. The next two days without a shirt would darken his naturally brownish toned skin until the Apache wouldn't know him from themselves. He was betting his life on the success of the deception.

That morning he had prepared his traveling gear, an old ammunition bag with a shoulder strap where he had placed five pounds of beef jerky. Wrapped in a cloth was a .45 caliber Derringer, the small handgun with two barrels. He had six extra rounds for the weapon, but he hoped he wouldn't have to use it. The knife on his belt was his only other weapon. His rifle would be in his way — it would be too heavy to carry and would slow him down — so he planned to leave it behind.

Back at the camp, Chisholm faded out of the desert toward the back of the major's tent. The camp didn't notice him. He peered around the side of the tent and watched the sentry who stood relaxed and bored in front of the tent flap. The sentry sighed and moved from one foot to the other. He saw only a blur in front of him, then a strong arm wrapped around his throat, his rifle had been knocked into the dust, and a knife was through his shirt just touching the skin over his heart.

"Major Black, sir, I think you'd better come out here a moment," the "Apache" called.

Major Black stepped through the flap of the tent, and his hand dug for his belted pistol then stopped.

His eyes flared, then he sobered. "Don't kill him. What do you want? Do you speak any English? *Habla Espanol?*"

The Apache relaxed his hold on the private and pushed him away, then watched the Major half draw his .45.

"Now, now, Major Black, don't be unfriendly. Indeed I do speak some English. I admit I don't talk as well as some of you, but then my early upbringing was educationally neglected. And after that it was all filtered through a magnificent Irish brogue."

"My God, it is you. Chisholm?"

"Right, Major. Just a little test to see if I could pass muster on my dye job and my Apache clothes."

Black chuckled. "I think I'd better give you an escort while you're in camp, or some trigger-happy trooper is going to gun you down. Damn. You could fool your best roundeye friend with that dye job." He sobered. "Good luck in the Superstitions. I have a hunch you're going to need it."

CHAPTER 5
DEATH SONG

It was on his second day in the Superstitions when Chisholm first saw the Apaches. Four braves rode along a ridge on strong Indian ponies and drove two mules and a yearling heifer ahead of them. They were five miles deeper into the Superstitions than the army patrol had penetrated. By the time Chisholm had scurried down two ravines and reached the ridge where the hostiles had been riding, dusk came and then quickly full darkness. He couldn't track them.

Chisholm thought how quickly he had reverted to his well-remembered Indian skills once he had entered the mountains. He had added his long knife to his weapons before he left the camp, strapping the makeshift scabbard across his back. The shortened cavalryman's sabre was positioned for a right-hand draw. He had cut down the blade to eighteen inches, and sharpened it on both sides of the new point so it would cut on either side. He left the ornate but practical brass handgrip and guard in place, and had been glad several times that it had been there.

The longknife was his trademark among the Apache, and he would wear it now only when there was no chance that he might be sighted and recognized by the locals. When he wanted to use it, the psychological value of it would be an important asset against the hostiles.

When Chisholm missed the party on the ridge line, and darkness came, he went down a steep draw to the Salt River and found a secluded clump of brush and small trees where he improvised a rough shelter and lay down on a bed of leaves. It was not cold, that was no problem in August in Arizona, even in the higher mountains where the temperature had been in the mid 70's both nights so far. It would remain about there well into October.

Chisholm lay in the leaves, blending with the ground and the foliage, and chewed on some jerky. He had spent many pleasant days and nights in these valleys and along the Salt River when he was growing up. Out here alone he could forget about the taunts, jeers and attacks by the Chiricahua boys.

He had found some edible berries that first day and he ate until he could hold no more just as he had done as a boy. Mother earth would shelter him, sister sky would watch over him and bring him the cool rains, brother sun would warm his days and turn the berries ripe and make the corn grow in the summer. He slept.

On the morning of the third day, Chisholm had just gained the high ridge to the left of the river and settled into his concealed lookout position, when he saw two parties of Apaches. One was made up of seven or eight persons, some children, and all walking a smaller ridgeline moving north and east, generally paralleling the route of the Salt River, yet to the west.

The second group was six braves, riding good Indian mounts and heading generally toward the Gila Valley. He guessed they were a raiding party. He was too far from either party to catch them, so he chose the one with the children to track. They must be coming from or going to one of the main camps.

Army Intelligence reported that there were four hundred Apaches hiding in the Superstition mountains. Chisholm knew the figure was high, perhaps twice too high, but he could not convince the colonel at Prescott who had hired him, nor had he been able to sway General Crook when they had talked. Two hundred Apaches of several tribes would be more accurate.

This was the first time he had seen squaws and children. That meant some kind of a camp must be nearby. As he followed the faint trail left by the moccasin-footed Apaches, he checked his own footwear. He had on moccasins of the Apache design. He had made them himself. They were the tenth or twelfth pair he had made in recent years to wear. Any Apache who looked at them would know they were authentic. It was another important part of his disguise.

Chisholm ran along the ridgeline at a ground-eating trot. He could keep up the speed all day if he had to. He cut the distance between himself and the band ahead quickly. Gradually he realized they might be heading to a familiar spot. Less than a mile ahead was a trail that led down into *rojo* canyon, which was a main tributary of the Salt. Down in the red canyon were some of the best blackberries and blueberries he had ever eaten. The band must be out berry picking for the tribe. If so, he was heading away from their camp, not toward it.

He wasted another hour confirming the

purpose of the squaws and the children. They had gone into *rojo* and he could see their baskets for the berries. At once Chisholm reversed his direction and tried to follow the tracks beyond where he had first found them. The mountain winds had whipped away some of the faint tracks, and less than a half mile from where he had doubled back, he lost the last of the trail sign.

Chisholm found a promontory and searched the vast area of peaks and ridges and the deepness of the Salt River gorge, but he could find no more sign of Apache.

The old summer camp! Perhaps they were camped there now. He remembered now where the tribe had moved one summer when some of the braves heard of a wandering band of buffalo and the hunters had charged off in wild excitement and expectations. It had been more than a dozen years since they had found any buffalo in the area. It turned out to be a false report, but the children had enjoyed the stay in the summer camp.

The Apaches hadn't been in hiding in those happier days, and for a month they enjoyed the lowlands, with the stream and the grass of summer and trees to play in.

Then with the coming of fall they had

traveled far to the south into the land of the Mexicans where they spoke only Spanish and traded with the Mexicans for corn and horses.

He would see if he could find the summer camp. Chisholm's moccasins sped over the familiar ground. He was remembering, adjusting his thinking from that of a boy of ten to his present view.

He found the double canyon off the Salt, then the twisted smoke tree and, almost as if it had been only yesterday, the small valley lay to his right hidden behind a screen of willow and cottonwoods. He moved cautiously into the trees, parted them carefully, moving like a Chiricahua, not making the slightest noise, not even stirring the silent warm air. At the last spray of leaves he looked into the valley. It was much smaller than he remembered, not over two hundred yards long, and half that wide, with a chattering stream that bubbled up from somewhere far below. The stream was what the Indians called "the never-ceasing waters." It flowed no matter how much or how little rain there was. The tribe's wise men said the waters came from far below in the center of mother earth where she stored the precious liquid for her chosen people, the Chiricahua.

Chisholm searched for the word to describe the wells. Artesian, a low-level artesian well where underground pressure forced the water upward. If it had any impurities in it they were filtered out through succeeding layers of soil. The water was pure, clear, and cold.

Nothing stirred in the summer camp's hidden valley. He checked every square foot of it, making sure there was no hidden brave stalking deer, for this was a favorite watering place for what little game there was in the region.

He saw nothing from his Indian eyes and ran into the open, his moccasins springing on the soft, lush grass of the meadow. It was as he remembered. The stream rose near the far end, flowed gently through the valley, spreading out and soaking into the thirsty soil as it went. Only a trickle managed to get to the far end where it was sucked up before it got past the screen of trees. Thus the valley protected itself from invaders.

Chisholm sat in the shade and chewed on jerky. The dried meat would be plenty to sustain him for the week. That and the berries and all the water he could drink.

He couldn't help but think how quickly life could change. It seemed only a few weeks ago that he had been here, laughing, crying, hiding, running, playing, as happy as he had ever been as an Apache. Now he hunted the Apache.

Was it tracking down his own people? Was he a traitor? It didn't feel that way. He was half Apache. There were many tribes in the nation such as the Apache Coyotero, but the Chiricahua and the Coyotero were constantly fighting, stealing horses and women. If cousins could fight, why not he, a half Apache? No, he had made that decision long ago when he began scouting. The raiding Apache must be rooted out and the killing of innocents stopped.

Apache scouts had been easy for the army to hire. Some of them spoke almost no English and came straight from the warpath. This was simply another way to fight against one of their natural enemies — another tribe of Apaches.

No, his half-Apache blood did not make him think of himself as a traitor. But first he had to find the Apaches. He had to discover their hiding and camping spots in places he could not remember or had no knowledge of.

The rest of the day he walked the ridges or lay in hiding watching known trails. Not once again that day did he see an Indian.

The morning of the fourth day Chisholm went back to watch the trail where he had lost the party of squaws and children. He watched for two hours by the sun, and was ready to leave when he heard laughter; then, along the trail, came two squaws and four children. Four young boys of ten or twelve were playing tricks on the squaws, but grudgingly following their orders. They came up that part of the trail where Chisholm had lost the tracks the day before. If he could follow them now they could lead him back to their camp. He should have no trouble; they were less than a hundred yards away.

Chisholm moved along behind them, careful to stay out of sight, but having to take chances now and then so he would not lose them. He had just passed an outcropping of rock that had concealed him and moved along the trail when, ahead of him, around a slight bend in the trail, came a Chiricahua brave. The brave stopped and stared hard at Chisholm. A lone hunter in search of food for his tipi, he wore only a pair of blue cut-off army pants and moccasins. Around his back was slung a loose short bow and a quiver of arrows. In his hand he carried a knife.

The brave advanced slowly, curiosity on

his face. He regarded Chisholm silently, paying close attention to the moccasins and buckskin leggings.

"Brother?" the Chiricahua said suspiciously. The knife came up, and he looked back down the trail.

"Of course, brother," Chisholm said in the Apache language.

"You are not of my tribe," the Apache snorted. "What tribe calls you brother?"

Chisholm knew then what he had to do; there could be no alarm. He smiled as he walked forward, moving lightly on the balls and toes of his worn moccasins, ready to take any needed evasive action. The scout walked up to ten feet of the brave and stopped as was the custom.

"I am a Mescalero Apache from the Rio Grande country, a shaman on a long journey to find the highest point in the Great Spirit's whole world. Look for the powerful spirits of the sun, the clouds and the rain so we may have good grass and that the squaws raise plenty of corn for the winter."

The Chiricahua brave frowned. He had never heard of the Mescaleros coming this far from their own lands. He would test the stranger.

"The Mescalero are no friends of the Chiricahua. Why should I allow you to walk the sacred Chiricahua lands?"

"We are brothers. Our father's fathers were brothers. We are a part of the great Apache nation. We no longer raid each other's villages."

"You lie, Mescalero," the Chiricahua spat. "You come sneaking along behind women and children. You seek out our camp so you can tell the blue coats. You are traitor!"

"I am Apache!"

"And I am Chiricahua! The Mescaleros killed my father in a raid only four moons ago!"

"I come in peace, a holy journey of a shaman, to appease the great spirits of the sun, the rain, and sky."

"You lie!"

"I have no bow to threaten you with."

"You have a knife, Mescalero! Use it!"

The brave lifted his own blade and danced forward. In one swift, sure move, Chisholm drew the short sabre from his back where the other man had not seen it. At once the brave's eyes widened, his mouth came open in soundless surprise.

"Longknife! A true traitor to his people. Now you will die. The half-man who rides with the hated blue coats. The half-woman who has changed his fire hair to black to fool us. You die!"

The Apache attacked, his short knife going against the 18-inch blade. He made no move to run away and string his bow so he would have a long-range advantage. He charged the longer weapon, knowing that he would be cut, but relying on his skill and ability to take a minor wound in order to deliver a fatal thrust.

The Chiricahua was a master with the blade, as Chisholm knew he would be when he attacked with the short weapon. He darted in, turned, feinted one way and slashed the other way with the blade. But Chisholm had learned his lessons well as an Apache child. He danced away from the cold steel and made no attempt to counterattack.

He waited. The Apache came at him again, stooping to grab a hand full of dust. Chisholm did the same and waited, his left arm outstretched. They circled on the trail, plunged into the top of a rocky ravine, worked back to the flatness of the trail, both feinting now, countering, staying at a distance, looking for a mistake, an advantage.

The other man was higher on the slope than Chisholm and he attacked quickly, darting down, throwing the dirt at Chisholm's eyes, then charging in at the moment the scout closed his eyes. The instant he sensed that the man had charged, Chisholm too threw his dirt. Both flailed with their weapons blindly during the few seconds. Each had covered his eyes with his hand and each man suffered a minor wound on that arm. Blood dripped from Chisholm's forearm where a deep, inch-long gash showed. The Apache had a slice on his shoulder, not deep but long.

"So we are bloodied. Now we fight like Apaches!" the brave challenged. He found a rock and hurled it at Chisholm, who dodged it and moved up the ravine. Chisholm attacked relentlessly now, driving the Apache backward, not allowing him time to reach for dust again, keeping him on the move defending against the longer weapon, leaping backward, staying out of range of the sharp sabre.

Then in his hurry, Chisholm stumbled. The Apache saw it, reversed his movement so quickly that he was on top of Chisholm before the scout hit the ground. The sabre came up in a reflex move and the blade caught the Apache as he surged forward. The weight of his body and his momentum rammed the blade between ribs and through a lung.

His force carried him over Chisholm, ripping the sabre from his hands. The knife in the Apache's hand trailing a slice across Chisholm's bare chest but not deeply. Chisholm ignored the wound, turned to the fallen brave and frowned.

The man lay gasping, the sabre extending from his chest. Both his hands were on it, holding the deadly steel.

"Don't pull it out," Chisholm said in Apache.

"I must. I must kill you," the brave whispered, his breathing labored and erratic.

"Your killing days are over. What is your name?"

"Lightning Two-Horn."

"Two-Horn, don't pull the blade out until you are ready to sing your death song. You know it is bad."

"I cannot live or die with the longknife in my chest. My spirit would forever be burdened with it." He was silent for a moment, then wailed. "Why does the sky grow dark in the morning?"

"A cloud, Two-Horn, nothing but a cloud."

"No, Longknife, it is not a cloud. It is the great spirit of death spreading his black wings over me. I should be on my promontory where I can sing my death song."

"I'll take you there, Two-Horn, I'll carry you."

"Why? Why would a traitor to his people help a brave? You are half roundeye, the Longknife all Apaches hate."

"I am half Apache, Two-Horn. Perhaps the best of me is Apache, who knows. I will carry you to your promontory."

"I have not selected one. I can see none. I am blind."

"Point to one, there are many nearby."

The Apache was quiet for a few moments, then he pointed. His finger angled toward a slight rise.

"Yes, I see it. I'll take you there. Think good thoughts — of cool mountain streams, of your woman, a successful hunt. It's going to hurt when I lift you."

"I am Apache, I feel no pain."

Two-Horn choked back a scream as Chisholm picked him up and carried him twenty yards to a crest on the trail. He lay him down gently. Two-Horn groaned then shook his head in anger.

The brave's half-closed eyes turned toward Chisholm.

"Longknife, you are a true Apache. I owe you a great favor for helping me. But it saddens me that I have no way to repay you. I will not kill you, that is my gift to you. Leave me now, I must be alone."

Without a word, Chisholm turned and

walked a hundred yards down the trail. The plaintive sound came to him, at first surprisingly strong and vigorous, then softer and softer until it became little more than a rattle. Two-Horn sang his Apache death song as his ancestors had done for hundreds of years. He told of the glorious days of battle against the roundeyes, and the Mescaleros, of his ritual when he became a man, of his love for his squaw, then of how he had left undone so many things. At last he spoke well of his tribe shaman and his family.

Suddenly even the rasping stopped. It did not end, Chisholm was sure of that. He had heard hundreds of death songs. He hurried to the spot and found Two-Horn staring blankly at the sun. The brave's hands held the sabre. With his last strength he had pulled the hated blade from his chest and it had killed him. Two-Horn had chosen his exact moment to die. But his spirit would not be burdened for eternity with a bluecoat's sabre buried in his chest.

Chisholm knew he should put Two-Horn into a tall tree, or leave him there on his promontory so his spirit would be able to leave his body easily and ascend into the heavens. But he could not. No one must find the body. He carried Two-Horn down the slope a hundred yards and laid him under a squaw bush so he could not be seen from the trail, or from overhead where the buzzards flew. Still it was a high enough point that the Indian's spirit would find it easy to fly out of his body and into the heavens.

Chisholm sat beside the body for ten minutes, realizing how quickly he had "gone back to the blanket" and become a Chiricahua again. But when any man died it was a special time. He was not ashamed of his Indian blood. Perhaps in time the roundeye would accept what was good and beautiful from the Indian. Perhaps, but not in his lifetime.

He also knew the looting, the killing, the stealing of women by the Apache had to end. The Chiricahua had stepped over the line from warfare to banditry; they were outlaws and lived by crime and murder. They must be stopped.

Even as he thought of it he began to chant. It was the traditional Chiricahua chanting wail for the dead, prayers that his spirit might waft quickly out of the danger of earth into the heavens of the happy hunting ground, where the plains were black with buffalo, where the deer spotted the valley, where the sweet rains came in the spring, where there was peace always, plenty of good food, and where the tipi was warm in the winter.

As he chanted, Wade Chisholm wept.

CHAPTER 6
BIG JIM CHISHOLM

The fourth day of his journey into the Superstitions ended shortly after Chisholm ended his death chant. He didn't have the heart to search out the trail any farther. He had a good idea now where it was, where it could lead. Instead he dropped down the ravine, went over one ridge and moved down to the lower reaches of the Salt River where he crossed and went back to his hidden valley. He tried to stay there each night now. It seemed safer, somehow, centrally located so it wasn't too far out of his way — and somehow it seemed like home.

He had not built a fire since he came into the mountains. He had no real need for one, except as recreation and for company on a lonely night. But he had to forego those small pleasures. As he ate his jerky that evening and watched the sun go down, he thought of the last summer he had spent with the Apaches.

He had been twelve that summer, bursting with energy and vitality and questions. He had asked his mother about everything and usually she would have the answers. Then one day he asked her where his father was. He knew the man's name was Big Jim Chisholm, that he was an Irishman, that he had lived with the Chiricahua for several years, and that he had red hair. But who was he? Where did he come from? How did he happen to live with the Apache?

"Mother, is it true that I had two fathers like the boys yell at me when they want to make me angry?"

Blue Feather had smiled at him and brushed back his red hair. The Apaches had called the boy Red Hair almost from the start and the name had stuck.

As the boy had looked up he realized that his mother was pretty, much prettier than any of the other Apache women he had seen. Her face was round and unblemished, her skin a soft, tawny brown, her cheek bones high under darting black eyes, and her unbraided black hair fell below her shoulders. She washed it twice a week as her husband had taught her, and combed it with the many combs he had brought her. Neither had she become fat like all of the other squaws. He knew that Blue Feather had been only fourteen when his father took her as his bride, with the blessings of the old Chiricahua chief, Hawk Killer.

Blue Feather had put down the doe skin she had been working on and told him to come sit beside her.

"Small man Red Hair, I think it is time you know about your great and good father. You are old enough now. Already you are starting to enter the rituals of manhood.

"You must remember that things were much different thirteen moons ago. We were not so shut off. We had whites come to our camps from time to time in peace. And we moved around a lot, usually to wherever game was plentiful. I was fourteen, a woman, and not yet given to any man.

"Then one day a white man suddenly came to our camp. We had been fighting with the Coyoteros and had our guards posted, yet this white man appeared at our inner camp. He was tall, taller than a young pine tree, and had hair the color of a *rojo* sunset, wide shoulders, a thick neck, and a very handsome face. What I liked about him was his laugh, a big laugh that he used a lot. Three of our braves drew knives, and one grabbed his rifle, but before any of them could attack, the stranger took off his gun belt and handed it and his rifle to a squaw.

Then he ignored the braves and walked to Chief Hawk Killer's tent and sat down beside him. The white man took a short peace pipe from his pocket, lit it, smoked and passed it to our brave chief."

"Why were our lookouts so foolish as to let a white-eye into our camp?" Red Hair asked his mother.

"They did not *let* him through. Like a spirit, he slipped past them. Even as they watched, he outwitted them. He was better at silent, unseen movement than even the Chiricahua. The braves didn't even know he had passed them.

"The chief and the braves were impressed by the courage of this roundeye who would walk into a Chiricahua camp and give up his weapons to a squaw. Then he began to talk with Spanish words, and Chief Hawk Killer understood him. The chief said since the Pine Tree Tall man was so brave, he would listen to what he said."

"And my father stayed and was a brave warrior, a brave fighter for the Chiricahua?" the young boy had asked.

"No, Red Hair. He was not a warrior, although he told Chief Hawk Killer that he could beat any of his braves in any feat of skill they wished to try. Even in fighting, as long as neither man was hurt. So they had contests. All day the braves took turns trying to defeat him. He was a good wrestler. He could throw a knife or an axe with greater skill than any of the braves. Only with the short bow did the braves defeat him. He stayed a week, and it was like a festival, a fiesta. At the end of the week, the Tall man with the red hair and Chief Hawk Killer held a long council around the fire. When it ended the two men smoked the peace pipe again and then went into the Chief's hut. They closed the flap and ate the sacred buttons from the peyote cactus. They did not come out for two days.

"They told later how they took long journeys in their minds, how they had wonderful dreams and thought they were flying over the world on the wings of eagles.

"When they came out of the hut they were blood brothers. Chief Hawk Killer called the tall man Red Hawk, and made him a blood brother Chiricahua. The Chief gave him every right and honor of a brave in the tribe.

"Two on the council objected. Both were jealous of Red Hawk, because they had never eaten the sacred buttons. Both challenged him to an Apache knife fight, with each man holding the end of a piece of cloth in his teeth. Red Hawk did not want to fight either man, but they made him. He took several cuts on his arms before he defeated the first brave, Long Eagle, and held his own knife to his throat signifying death. Long Eagle was beaten and disgraced. He was dishonored and forced to leave camp. But at least he was still alive.

"Standing Horse, the other brave, was a much better knife fighter than Long Eagle, and Red Hawk had at last to kill him to save his own life.

"Soon, others in the camp learned what Red Hawk had told the chief. Red Hawk was a gold man, he searched for the worthless squaw clay, the soft golden metal that was good for nothing. He was free to roam the Superstitions hunting for gold. He would be safe. He was a Chiricahua! So he went into the mountains and searched and came back. After his first trip he chose me, Blue Feather, as his bride. I moved into his hut and I was happy because he had chosen me.

"For three moons we were happy. The tribe stayed in the mountains, and the second year you were born. You were strong and healthy. Your father named you, but I couldn't remember it. His name was Big Jim Chisholm, so for a while I called you Little Red, but the Indian name soon was used. Red Hair became your name and so that is what I call you.

"Your father found little gold, which disappointed him, but he kept looking. He took part in the tribal work, but went on no raids or in any war parties. He did hunt and fish; he brought in his share of food for the tribe.

"Then one day in the spring he went looking for gold again. This time he sent back a report with a passing hunter that he had found a big amount of gold, a tremendous wall of gold that the sun glinted off in the afternoon and dazzled everyone who looked at it.

"But when the hunter went back to him with the provisions he asked for, Big Jim Chisholm was dead. He had been tortured before he died — Indian torture. In the sand, in several places, was the picture name of the killer. It was Long Eagle, the brave your father had disgraced and let live. Your father thought he knew the Chiricahua, but he didn't. Long Eagle had been banished, but he stayed in the mountains, waiting for his chance to find Big Jim Chisholm alone so he could capture him and torture him to death.

"Your father was buried in the highest tree in all the land, and his spirit surely floated free and into the sky. Since then, I have worked as other widows do, begging for food for both of us, picking berries to trade for meat, trapping birds and rabbits when I can. And all the time I taught you every Apache skill your father would have taught you." She smiled tenderly at him and with her hand she smoothed out his unruly red hair. "Soon you will be a man, my son. Soon you will build shelter and bring food for both of us."

Less than a week after the talk with his mother, young Chisholm had watched a Chiricahua war party return to camp. The young warriors had raced their ponies from one end of the camp to the other, yelping in triumph, holding up scalps of yellow, brown, and black hair. Their raid had been on a town at the edge of the Gila Valley. It had been a massacre, a tremendous victory for the Apache. Only one brave had been wounded, and the war party had brought back ten horses, three beef cows, and two cows that would give milk. For three days there had been great joy and feasting in Red Hair's village.

The Chiricahuas had felt safe in their mountain retreat. Semi-permanent huts had been built a half-mile inside the Superstitions, in a small branch valley along the Salt

River. No white man had ever dared follow an Apache into this place. The land was sacred, protected by the Great Spirit, a place of death for invaders.

Then, at sunrise one morning a week after the raid on the town, Blue Feather and Red Hair had awoken to the sounds of rifle fire and people screaming — and the acrid smell of gunsmoke. Red Hair had run outside and was immediately caught up in chaos. Half the village huts were on fire; soldiers were charging their mounts through the village; Apaches ran in every direction, some screaming in fear, others cursing in anger, and still others silently falling in death. Rifles spat death, silver sabres lashed out mercilessly, and thundering horses trampled all in their way.

Then, as suddenly as it had begun, the attack was over. Forty-two braves were dead or wounded. Fifteen squaws had been killed and another dozen lay writhing on the ground. Twenty children and infants lay crushed and dead. Only five squaws and eight children survived the holocaust unscathed. And they were terrified, running about, looking for their husbands and sons, their daughters, their mothers and fathers. The sound of weeping and chanting soon filled the air.

Blue Feather had been cut down by two bullets as soon as she had stepped from her hut. The first bullet had plowed into her right shoulder, driving her backwards; the second bullet, the deadly one, had slammed into her forehead, exiting the back of her head, blasting out a handful of bone and flesh and brain. The woman had gone down without a sound.

Red Hair had been struck in the side by a wild-swinging sabre and had collapsed in shock about twenty feet from his hut. The boy strained to clear his senses and looked up just in time to see his mother gunned down. He had cried out his disbelief, then, in terrible pain, he had dragged himself to his mother's body and wept bitterly. The only person in the world he truly loved was dead. As he lovingly touched the stilled lips, his grief increased in intensity. He cried for his mother and himself. He was frightened and alone. After several minutes, physically and emotionally drained from his wound and his grief, he had lain his head on his mother's breast and slipped into unconsciousness.

The red hair of one of the Indian captives had stood out and, at first, the soldiers thought they had rescued a captured white boy. The troop's commanding officer, Captain Donald Barr, had pulled Red Hair away from the other Chiricahuas for questioning.

"Well, what have we here, a white boy?" the captain said kindly.

Red Hair examined the white bandage that covered his wound, then stared his hate at Barr.

"Tell me, son, can you speak English?"

Barr extended his arm in a friendly gesture and Red Hair promptly bit the man's hand.

"Damn!" Barr swore, yanking his hand back.

A grimy, very tired-looking corporal, his right arm in a sling, suddenly stepped forward and belted Red Hair with his good hand. The boy went down.

"Jeffers!" snapped the captain.

The corporal glared at the captain. "I heard 'bout this 'un, Cap'n. That red hair don't make him white. He's Injun through to his gut. Better'n he be dead."

Barr nodded. "I know what you're telling me, Corporal, but he's still just a boy — and right now he's my responsibility."

Red Hair's narrowed eyes swung from the corporal to the captain as Barr, holding his wounded hand, once again advanced on him.

"*Se habla Espanol?*" he asked Red Hair,

again in a kindly tone.

The boy stared at him for a moment, then suddenly leaped forward and began beating his fists on Barr's chest. "You murderers!" he screamed. "You kill women and children! You are not men! You are worse than the coyote! You killed my mother!"

Again, Corporal Jeffers lashed out, and again the boy went down. Captain Barr studied Red Hair for a long moment, then sighed and walked away.

When they had ridden away from the death camp, Red Hair had been tied to a horse. Along with the rest of the Chiricahuas, he was taken into Gila Valley and eventually he had ended up in a stockade in Prescott.

The boy's red hair continued to set him apart from the other prisoners. The women and children who had survived the attack were soon transported to a reservation, but Red Hair remained confined to the stockade. But Captain Barr kept talking to the half-breed, and gradually won his confidence and, eventually, his friendship. By the time Red Hair Chisholm was thirteen, everyone in the Arizona Territory knew his story.

He was paroled into Captain Barr's custody and took up residence in the captain's home. Barr was married and had two sons, both younger than Red Hair. The young half-breed learned English quickly, and within a half-year of his capture was attending the fort's school.

The boy showed an amazing capacity for learning, and Captain Barr and his wife, Virginia, traded off nights helping him with his studies. It was Virginia's idea to have him legally renamed Wade Chisholm and that's what he was called in school.

Wade did so well in the post school that soon he was helping the teacher with the younger students. In his fourth year at the school the teacher became ill, and Wade took over as the new teacher. It was during that time that Wade came to the attention of General Wesley Merritt, who championed him for an appointment to West Point. Some neatly done sleight of hand concealed the fact of Chisholm's Indian blood and his mother was listed as Heather Canzonari. Her Italian dark good looks resulted in his coloring.

He flourished in West Point, graduated near the middle of his class and he was thought of as a black Irishman with a sense of humor.

After West Point, General Merritt made a place for him on his staff and soon promoted him to captain over the heads of a hundred other officers in the field. It stirred a controversy, and Chisholm asked for duty fighting Indians in southwest Arizona Territory. The hard duty on the frontier was granted. For three years he took the worst jobs the army could give him and handled them well.

Then came the controversy at Swallow River Camp. After its ensuing series of events, Chisholm resigned his commission under an unfavorable cloud. However, no formal charges were ever filed. But it left him in an impossible situation that not even his friend, General Merritt, could unscramble for him.

For a year Wade tried to live in the east, working in a business outfitting travelers for trips to the west. But Arizona was in his blood. A year after he left, Wade Chisholm returned to the Territory and signed on as a scout for the U.S. Army. Once again he settled into the country and the work that he knew the best.

Chisholm turned over on his leaf-and-bough bed deep in the Superstition Mountains and stared up at the brilliant Arizona stars. He shouldn't be thinking about the past. It was gone, over with. He had to think about the here and now, his future. Right now he had a job to do, to find the base camp of the Chiricahua Apaches. The raids against the innocent settlers had to be stopped. And that meant that it was up to him to show the army where the Apache fortress was.

Wade rolled over again, heard a night animal in the brush and remained quiet. Out of the night came the form of a two-fork buck walking directly toward him, the wind at the buck's back. The deer stepped over the quiet loglike form on the ground and only then picked up the scent of a human. The graceful animal bounded away in a smooth twenty-foot jump, hit on all four legs, and jumped again another twenty feet before disappearing into the blackness.

Chisholm smiled, turned over, and drifted off to sleep.

Chapter 7
The Eagle's Nest

Chisholm was up at dawn, anxious to get started on his mission. He washed in the bubbling stream, shook out his wet hair, then ate half his day's ration of dried jerky before going up the trail along the Salt River at a trot. He wasn't running and he wasn't walking, but he would cover twenty miles on foot faster than a cavalry troop could walk their mounts the same distance.

He came to his usual trail up to the ridges on the west side of the river, and this time changed his mind in mid-stride and crossed the stream and went up a ravine that would lead him to the east side of the Salt. The cliffs were just as high as the places he had been previously; they towered 1200 feet over the water below. Perhaps what he needed in his search was a change of scenery, a different approach, the way they had taught him problem-solving in that tactics class at West Point. He smiled. It had been a long time since he had thought about any of the studies at the military academy. It had been a good education for him, and he was properly thankful, even if the Army had turned out to be a personal disaster.

He slowly worked his way up the canyon; the going was harder for there was no trail here. His moccasins soon wore through in one spot and he could feel his bare foot on the rocks. He would find some tree bark to insert in the leather, or perhaps some hardy leaves of a river plant.

For now, he kept moving. He gained the top of the first ridge, turned up it, and went through a shallow valley and up another ridge that led closer to the river.

An hour later he rested on the highest point he had found along the edge of the gorge. It had to be a thousand feet to the water below. The river sparkled in the shafts of sunlight just slanting into the bottom of the gorge.

He lay on a typical nearly treeless mountain of central Arizona, where the sugaro cactus are the largest living plants, and clumps of mesquite and chaparral cluster in small washes and ravines. The gorge here was a quarter of a mile wide, where the crooked Salt River had carved down through the various strata of rock haphazardly over the previous centuries.

At this point the east side of the gorge could be walked down easily; it lay in gentle sweeping slopes. But on the other side a pair of sharp sheer cliffs rose well over 1200 feet. He lay just below the ridgeline, so he would not silhouette himself against the sky, and stared across the gorge. Why had the Apache been using the ridges so much? Why not the easier routes along the river below? The Chiricahua were not known to take a longer trail when a shorter one was available. Why the ridges?

Soon he would return to the ridge where Two-Horn had died, and he would follow that trail. He was more sure than ever now that the squaws had been returning to their camp.

Chisholm let the sun lull him into near sleep as he lay there, watching the ridges across the way.

He had played and roamed over this land when he was ten years old, but they seldom went to the top of the mountains. There was nothing up there. The game, the fish, the birds, and the water were all in the canyon below. Why scale the rocky heights?

But things must have changed. Now the Apaches were up here. Why?

For a moment he thought he saw movement on the slopes across the gorge. He discounted it, then rubbed his eyes and shaded them with his hand as he looked again, concentrating on the exact spot. Yes, there was movement. Mountain goats? Possibly. There were still many goats foraging about in the hills.

He let his eyes sweep across the area, watching for nothing in particular, but sweep-recording everything. The spots moved again, not as mountain goats, not with irregular jumps, but with the steady progress of human beings on a narrow trail. As Chisholm concentrated on the largest dot against the sheer rock wall, he saw that it was moving forward steadily. There was some kind of a *trail* along the face of the cliff! He looked again, not believing what he thought he had seen. But it was not a sheer rock wall, rather there was a seam where one sheet of rock face met another, a crease, where there must be room enough to move along carefully. There was a trail. He watched again, but the lead figure vanished into a crevice and he couldn't make out where it had gone to.

He knew he had to get a closer look, yet without the figures on the trail spotting him. He scurried back over the brow of the ridge-line and trotted back down the slope of the ravine he had used to climb up this way. He made good time and came out a half mile downstream from where he had seen the figures. Crossing the river on a sand bar, Chisholm found enough protection under the bank so he could work along the shallows of the river the half mile upstream, then taken another look at the cliff.

The water was cool where he was forced to wade it at several spots, but soon he was at the gully he wanted and worked up it beside a cone-shaped hump in the rock formation. The trail was somewhere above, far above, but he would have a good view of it. Chisholm edged around a rock shelf and stared at the slope. The last of the dots was there, much larger now, probably a small boy. He walked with the care-free spirit of his age, peering over the edge from time to time but showing no fear. He walked along what seemed to be a two- or three-foot wide trail. Chisholm could not see where the trail led, but it had leveled out and was continuing parallel to the water, which was seven hundred feet below.

Chisholm had seen enough. That was why the Apaches were on the ridges. They didn't live in the valley anymore. They must have found an inaccessible valley or meadow high up somewhere. Another artesian spring perhaps brought water up to them. He moved quickly now, scrambling back to the river in the protection of the rocky ledges and crumbling granite and basalt piles of rock they called mountains.

He moved with a new purpose. Now he had two possibilities. The trail the squaws and boys had taken was aimed in the same direction as those Indians he had just seen. Was it possible it was part of the same trail? He would have the answer to that question when he climbed to the top of the ridge and followed both trails.

As he trotted down the path along the Salt River, he worked out his strategy. He would wait until almost dark to attempt to follow anyone along that ledge. In the darkness there would be fewer Apaches moving, and he would have time to work along the trail slowly, carefully. He had no wish to meet a Chiricahua brave on that trail coming from the other way.

It was after midday when he found the trail near where Two-Horn had died. Cautiously, he followed it and found new tracks on top of the older ones. Again, some were made by adult moccasins, some by children's. As he moved north he felt the trail climbing again, and soon it left the ridge-line and angled toward the gorge. Now it was less a trail than the side of a mountain, and he had to watch closely to determine where the Apache feet had trod.

Soon he came to a more defined trail, where pebbles and rocks had been kicked away and a smooth path showed. The trail turned again toward the gorge, and suddenly he came to a shallow arroyo that fell away toward the river. The trail used it for a hundred yards and he saw where it came to an abrupt drop off. Before that point the trail swung to the left. Chisholm looked down and could see the water in the gorge.

If he went any farther in the daylight he knew he would be easy to see from several directions. He needed the cover of darkness. There were no trees or brush here, only the usual rocky hills with sparse grass and a few wild flowers and cactus. The sugaro cactus rose fifteen, sometimes twenty, feet; they were the tallest plants in the land. He backtracked fifty yards and found a crevice to his right. From it, he could be in partial shade; he could hide, blend in with the rocks. If anyone approached he would freeze against a rock and stay that way without moving for five minutes or an hour, whatever was required.

This would serve as a hiding spot. The sun was still high, perhaps at two o'clock, when he settled into the shade of his crevice and began his long wait. Chisholm was curious who might be passing this way, because now he was convinced that this was the same trail he had seen from the other side of the gorge, where the Apaches were moving to their secret stronghold.

The scout rested, his eyes not closed, yet he was as close to sleep as he could get. The slightest motion or sound brought him alert at once. A cottontail rabbit nibbled on some sparse shoots of grass which had sprouted since the last shower. It hopped around ten yards in front of Chisholm, not knowing he was there. The scout also saw a big hawk circle, then work closer, moving in on the rabbit from behind. Now he saw it was a bald eagle, that descended in tight, quiet circles until it was less than twenty feet above the nibbling cottontail.

With a sudden, wings-folded dive, the eagle slashed down through the sky, threw out its wings at the last moment to slow its dive, as talons almost as big as a man's hand hit the rabbit, grabbed hold, and held on. The eagle's four-foot wings beat the air furiously. The rabbit gave a startled death cry as the strong talons closed around its throat and then the big bird was airborn again, wings churning the sky as it rose higher and higher. It circled once, then landed on a small shelf atop a sheer twenty-foot slab of a rocky spire.

Chisholm smiled grimly. It had been at least a dozen years since he had sat in the wilderness and watched nature in action, since he had seen larger, smarter animals kill smaller ones. He had just witnessed one of the cleverest predators in the world. And the eagle had no enemies; no other animal hunted it for food.

Before he had finished the thought he heard someone on the trail. Two squaws came along, each carried a machete. On the back of each woman, tied carefully with strips of rawhide, rested a four foot stack of closely packed firewood. Most of it was dead cactus, the rest dry brush from the river below.

Chisholm let out a long-held breath as they passed. Two tests were over. The women had not seen him crouched in the crevice. Nor had he recognized either of the women. He had been worried that he might know some of the Apaches he would find. He had grown up with this band to the age of twelve, and even though that had been fourteen years ago he should still recognize most of them. But then what boy of twelve paid that much attention to ugly old squaws of twenty-five or thirty years?

He was sure he would know many of them, especially the men when he came close enough. He did not know Two-Horn, but that didn't worry him. The brave could have come from another tribe, or he could have changed enough growing up so that Chisholm would have failed to identify him. Later, he might have to deal with this problem.

The load of wood filled in the last bit of evidence that he needed. This indeed was the trail to the Apache hideout. They had to carry wood into the camp for their fires. But it could still be in a remote valley or meadow or a small ravine where the Chiricahua had found shelter.

Now all he had to do was wait for darkness and then creep closer, identifying the camp for sure before he made his way back to the cavalry near Phoenix.

In spite of his good intentions, Chisholm dozed. The sun had progressed and now slanted in on his legs and chest. He splashed dust from the ground over his legs and moccasins so they would blend better. He studied the trail and waited.

It was nearly four, by the position of the sun, when Chisholm heard noises, the unmistakable sound of someone sobbing. It was a woman.

A few moments later he felt the tread of unshod Indian ponies on the hard ground. He had not noticed hoofprints before on the trail. Many moccasins would blot out the hoofprints quickly. He edged back deeper into the cleft, wishing now that he was farther than fifty feet from the trail.

The lead horse carried a Chiricahua brave, but Chisholm could see only the side of his face and then his back. He did not know the man. Another pony came and Chisholm slid around the edge of the rock a few inches so he could see the rest of the party. Six horses, all unshod. The third rider from the front was a white woman. She had long brown hair and was tied to the horse where she sat astride a blanket. She wore a gingham print skirt but was nude to the waist. Her head hung down, eyes closed and she cried.

Chisholm flinched at the appearance of the girl, wanting to charge out and rescue her, to take her back to her family, to cover her. But he knew it would be foolish. She was young and pretty, not over seventeen or eighteen, he guessed, slender with a narrow waist and full, outthrust breasts.

He became one with the rocks as the last

in the line of horses passed. After seeing the girl he had not looked at the other braves. He did not want to find out if he knew any of them or not, because they were murderers, he was sure. The girl's family must have been slaughtered. His hand tightened around a rock and he felt his anger rising.

The next three hours passed slowly, then at last it was dusk. There would be a good moon tonight, it would help him see as he climbed along the trail. There had been no more Indians on the path. He hoped they were all in the stronghold celebrating.

As dusk deepened he came away from the rocks, stretched to loosen his unused muscles, then walked along the trail, slowing when it became treacherous. Soon he was well beyond where he had been before. The path slanted toward the gorge again, and this time rose over a notch of land, then went down into the edge of a ravine where there was a smattering of brush.

He heard movement ahead and crept up cautiously. An Indian boy tied the last horse to a ground stake, then hurried away up the trail. Twelve horses, a milk cow, and two mules stood in the makeshift enclosure. There seemed little for them to graze on, but he smelled a fresh spring closeby, and he saw a blush of grass which would provide a little grazing for the animals.

When he was sure there was no one else at the site, he moved across the small pasture and found the trail. Here it swung directly toward the face of the cliff. It must have been this section he had seen from across the gorge.

The trail was narrow, less than a foot wide in some spots, but in those spots the wall slanted back enough so that even the fat squaws could walk past. The trail was not dangerous unless he tried to hurry. Chisholm moved cautiously, watching for his next step, and in places he saw where hammers and some kind of steel chisel had been used to cut away more of the loose rock to allow for easier passage. The trail widened for a while, then narrowed to a few inches as the wall slanted nearly straight upward. He pressed onward, then paused and looked ahead. For a moment he saw the flickering of firelight reflected from some rocks, and he was curious. Why would the Apache build an open fire?

Again the trail slanted downward. He was well below the top of the cliff now. How could there be a meadow or valley in such a position? It baffled him, but at the same time, he reasoned that this was why the stronghold had remained a secret for so long.

The trail was easier now, slightly wider, and he moved at a fast walk until the path went down steeply and he saw a turn ahead. He moved to the bend in the trail and peered cautiously around it. Even before that he had heard excited voices, shouts, laughter, and some singing.

Some forty yards ahead he saw a cave. It lay in a nook at another sharp turn in the trail. A cave! The Chiricahua were hiding in a cave on this sheer bluff overlooking the Salt River gorge. An excellent defensive position, Chisholm thought.

He marveled at the ingeniousness of the Apache. He had to get closer. He estimated that he had come down five hundred feet from the top of the bluff, but that he was still seven hundred feet from the water far below. There was no way up to the cave from the gorge. It was an ideal stronghold.

Fires flickered near the mouth of the cave. It was what he had seen from above. There was a small flat area at the mouth that became little more than a widening of the trail, and on the other side it fell away in a sheer drop of hundreds of feet. In the dancing light of the flames, he saw that at the cave mouth itself there was a natural parapet of smooth stone that rose ten feet, blocking the interior from view and affording natural protection. It looked impregnable.

Chisholm eased around the corner of the rock and worked his way closer. He had seen no guards. By the time he was within twenty yards of the cave he could see down into a section of the mouth in front of the stone wall. Several warriors had lit a fire and were obviously celebrating their raid and the new slave. The girl was paraded around, naked, her hands tied behind her back. The warriors were singing and tipping bottles, which made Chisholm guess that the raiding party had found the rancher's liquor supply and brought most of it back as well as the slave.

How many Apaches were in the cave?

That was his next question. And how could he rescue the girl? He knew it was foolish even to consider it. He had found out what he came to discover. He had completed his job, and now should turn and ride for the bivouac. But he couldn't. He had seen more than one young white girl brought into the Chiricahua camp. Unless a chief chose her for his squaw, she was the property of the man who caught her. He could use her any way he wanted to.

If he tired of her sexually, he could loan

her to sleep with his friends, he could kill her, he could use her for knife throwing practice, or he could refine his skills of torture on her. No white girl he remembered had lasted more than three weeks in the Chiricahua camp when he was growing up. He didn't understand it then, and he barely did now, but he could not accept it.

He had to get the girl away from them.

Perhaps he could, if they were drunk enough. He would wait. For an hour he watched the cave entrance and all the hiding spots around the cave. He saw no guards; he watched and listened to the Indians getting drunker by the minute.

Chisholm guessed they must have begun drinking as soon as the braves had returned. After three hours they should be so drunk they would pass out. The squaws would go to sleep, too, in relief that no one was killed in a sudden drunken fight. The children would be far in the rear of the cave, protected and sleeping. But where would they have the white girl?

Chisholm guessed that she would be beside the brave who captured her. He was a hero, a glorious warrior. He would keep her as long as he could. The young boys who had not been permitted to drink would be the most dangerous ones; they would lie awake as long as they could, listening.

The scout rose from where he lay and walked slowly, a little drunkenly, toward the cave. He was in plain sight now, and if any guard or lookout saw him, the die would be cast. But he expected no lookouts. The tribe was hidden, invulnerable.

Two minutes later he crouched at the rocks just below the entrance to the cave. He unstrapped the long knife from his back and left it. The sabre would give him away instantly. Now he was just another Chiricahua who had had too much firewater.

Lurching and staggering, he gained the entrance to the cave and quickly looked around. Two braves had passed out near the lip of the cliff, a broken whiskey bottle between them. They would not move until morning. Another brave had fallen behind the parapet wall. Inside the cave opening only one fire burned, but it lit up the whole area. The girl was not near the front. He staggered over bodies and saw one squaw sit up, then burp and fall back to the ground. There were about twenty braves at the front of the cave and all were either sleeping or drunk and unconscious.

At the far side of the cave he saw the white girl. She had been tied, both hands in front of her, and then tied on a rawhide rope that went around the waist of her captor.

He had to make it look convincing that the girl had escaped. When he came to her, he saw that the girl was still awake, eyes staring straight ahead, dull, but not the total glaze he had feared.

He bent beside her, put his hand over her mouth and felt her struggle. His lips moved close to her ear.

"No. Don't fight me. I'm here to help you. I'll help you escape. Get away. You understand?"

Her blue eyes widened, then she nodded. He moved his hand, then his knife slashed the rawhide holding her wrists. He saw now that she wore the gingham skirt but nothing else. Chisholm found a blue blouse and another skirt the Indians must have brought back in the raid.

He cut the line to her captor, then took a fist-sized rock and slammed it down across the forehead of the brave who had captured her. He wanted to kill him, but the girl probably could not do that in an escape. It had to look normal. The brave half sat up, groaned and sank back, a bloody trail across his forehead.

The white girl moved with him as they stepped over the drunken bodies. He had not made a count. More than fifty he was sure. Perhaps twice that many. At the parapet he helped the girl put on the shirt, then told her to take off the gingham skirt.

She frowned.

His whisper came too loudly. "We must make them think you tried to get away and fell over the side, that you are dead."

She nodded, stepped out of the skirt and put on the other one showing no embarrassment. She was well beyond that state; all she was trying to do was stay alive.

He led her down the return trail half way to the bend, then ran back and ripped the gingham skirt in half, snagging part of it over the edge of the drop-off, and throwing in the other half over the side. He made claw marks on the edge of the sandy soil, then stepped over them, picked up his long knife and strapped it in place, then ran down the trail to the girl.

Chisholm knew that he shouldn't talk to her yet; she would only begin crying and that might bring some of the young men. He warned her to be quiet as they moved away, and it wasn't until they arrived at the horses that he let her talk.

Instead she cried, falling on him, putting her arms around him and sobbing. When she finished, he found two lengths of raw-hide rope and quickly fashioned two war bridles for the ponies. These he made by putting two half hitches around the horses' lower jaws, with the ends of the rope going on each side of the neck to the rider. It made an effective yet simple bridle.

"Can you ride?" Chisholm asked her.

She nodded.

He helped her mount and they turned the horses up the trail. Chisholm was not sure how to get out the fastest way, but he decided he would swing down to the Salt River as soon as he could.

About a half hour later, he estimated they were eight or nine miles into the gorge. The girl trailed behind him, riding well. She was alert, but frightened, and periodically looked behind her to see if they were being followed. Chisholm understood her fear; he knew it might take her months to get over the horror of being a Chiricahua captive, even though they had had her for only one day. He had seen this fear on white captives before.

Chisholm began trying for better time. They had to be well out of the Salt River gorge by daylight or they'd risk the chance that the Apaches would catch them. He and the girl needed time, time to put a lot of miles between them and the Apache. He hoped that when the Indians woke up their hangovers would be so bad they wouldn't immediately notice the girl was missing. Or, if they did, that they'd believe the signs he left, that she had fallen over the side of the cliff.

Of course, he knew that as soon as the Apaches discovered two horses missing, the game would be up and they'd be after them. This thought spurred him into increasing his pace, urging the girl to keep up with him.

Chisholm now regretted he had left his rifle behind. He had only the long knife and the six rounds for his Derringer. He sighed and urged his mount forward. All he could do was hope they'd have the time to get away.

CHAPTER 8
A WOMAN'S WAYS

At most places they could do little but let the trailwise ponies pick out their own path over the downslopes and the ridges in the darkness of the night. Chisholm knew he could make better time on foot, and hoped that a dozen sober Chiricahua braves were not at that very minute running along after them.

They progressed steadily, moving the horses faster where they could. The girl was a good rider; she kept up with him, her fear motivating her to take chances every now and then.

It took them over an hour to work down to the Salt River. Then they walked the horses in the shallows for a quarter of a mile before they came out on the firm trail and he set a faster pace downstream.

They were still a half mile inside the canyon when the first streaks of dawn broke over the ridges. Chisholm pulled up the horses and let them drink. He sat almost knee to knee with the girl and she watched him, fear still tinging her face.

"Miss, I think I should explain. I'm not Apache, at least half of me is not Apache. I'm Wade Chisholm, a scout attached to the 5th U.S. Cavalry out of Prescott. I was on a scouting mission into the hills and saw the Apaches bring you into camp last night."

"Oh." It was the first word she had said. She shuddered and tears sweeped from her eyes. "Thank you . . . I. . . ."

"You don't have to say anything, Miss. We're not out of this yet. We've got a lot of hard riding to do and without saddles. I'm afraid I've gotten soft and used to the leather these last few years." He pulled up his mount's head. "We better go. We can talk again when it's safer."

They rode for three hours, pushing the mounts as much as Wade thought they could without hurting them, realizing they had to make the mounts last all the way to Phoenix.

Ever since they had left the gorge and angled toward the tiny settlement, Chisholm had kept an eye on their back trail and on the edge of the Superstitions. But no where did he see any signs of riders following them, or trying to angle across their path.

They may have done it: escaped from the Chiricahuas. It wasn't done often. Either the Indians were still too hung-over from their bout with the whiskey, or the man who captured the girl was too sick to go chase her down, or his ardor had cooled. Perhaps the glory of the capture had been enough for him and he didn't want to bother with her any more. Maybe. Chisholm kept watching for the next hour. When he saw nothing to indicate any chase, he eased up beside a small patch of grass and brush along the river and slid from his mount.

"Let's rest here for a while," he said.

The girl slid off the horse and sighed, stretching out on the grass in total relaxation for a few seconds. Then she sat up quickly, eyes wary, suspicious.

He had both horses, letting them drink from the narrowing flow of the Salt River, where it came into the thirsty desert.

"What's your name?" he asked.

"Hannah," she said, some of the fear subsiding. "Hannah Miller, I live with my parents over. . . ."

"You don't have to talk about it. Look, I'm going to wash up a little. There's a pool down there that's screened if you want to use it. I've got some berry juice dye I want to see if I can get out of my hair." He didn't wait for her to make up her mind. He went to the pool, kicked off his moccasins, and waded into the cool waters. For ten minutes he scrubbed at the dye in his hair, then he washed the desert dirt from his arms and chest before he came out of the stream. He had not taken off his pants and the leggings. They would dry quickly.

As he shook out his hair and slanted the water from it, he heard a sound behind him and spun around.

Hannah stood in front of him, her skirt and blouse in a pile on the ground beside her. He couldn't help but stare for a moment at her slender young body, with the small waist, full breasts and slender legs. She was a tall girl, about five feet six. She watched him with a serious expression.

"Mr. Chisholm, I know you saved my life. I had given up, totally. I owe you more than I can ever repay, but I thought perhaps as a start I could do this, let you . . . you know."

He stood and touched her shoulders, then kissed her gently on the cheek.

"Hannah, you are the most beautiful woman I've ever seen, the most desirous, and enticing. But you don't owe me a thing. I did what I had to do. I lived with the Chiricahua tribe for twelve years when I was growing up. I know what they do to captive women. I couldn't let them do that to you. Now dress quickly, we must be moving again. We still have a long ride."

She hadn't moved. Now she stepped closer to him. "Are you sure? The Indians didn't . . . didn't touch me. They made me walk around naked to shame me. Nobody raped me. Not even the brave who evidently owned me. He was waiting, I think, until today."

"I'm glad, Hannah, that they didn't hurt you. But right now we do have to ride, there's no time. Please dress."

She bent and picked up the skirt, put it on slowly, then the blouse, at last buttoning the front of the shirt.

"Did much of the brown dye come out of my hair?" he asked. She looked at him, surprised at the question. She sighed and there was a touch of relief showing in her face.

"The color? What color was it?"

"A few days ago it was red."

"Oh, now it's reddish brown, but more brown."

"I'll have to buy a hat."

They rode.

No one followed them. An hour later they

walked the Indian ponies into the village of Phoenix. There was only one small general store in the town, and Chisholm rode up to the back door, tied the horses and went inside with the girl.

Josh McCurdy squinted through metal-rimmed spectacles.

"What in tarnation is this, some kind of Indian raid? If I didn't know better I'd say it was Captain Chisholm himself. But the gent by that name I know got himself a head full of bright red hair. Who in tarnation are you, sir?"

Chisholm grinned. "And the scoundrel who runs this nest of rattlesnake tails used to be a friend of mine. If he's still around, you let me know."

The two men shook hands firmly, grinning like a pair of newly rich prospectors.

"It's been two years since I seen you, Chisholm, you polecat. What happened to the red hair?"

"Oh, the army. They decided red hair was against regulations. Hey, you still have women's clothes in this rat's nest?" Then he turned, remembering the girl. "Oh, Josh, this is Miss Hannah Miller, Hannah, this is Josh McCurdy." They both nodded.

"Josh, how many favors do you owe me now?"

"Several, Captain, several."

Chisholm spelled it out quickly. He wanted the merchant to outfit Miss Miller with suitable clothes, then pack her a suitcase with more clothes and whatever else she wanted. Then he wanted him to find her a place to stay for a week or so.

Josh listened without comment and, when Chisholm was through giving instructions, he pulled a small suitcase and a carpet bag out of his stock.

"No problem with the clothes and things. The Missus saw to it that we got all the female necessities. Never sell many, but we got them. About a place to stay. Miss Miller can stay with us for a while. We got that extra bedroom now that Milly is gone, and Martha is lonesome most of the time."

"Thnaks, Josh. I appreciate that. And no questions. If anyone asks, the lady came in from Prescott and will be moving on in a month or so."

"Right," Josh said. He gave Hannah the suitcase. "Here, Miss Miller, you just pick out what you want, no rush."

Back at the counter, Josh uncorked a bottle of whiskey and offered it to Chisholm. The scout tipped it and drank, then wiped his lips.

"Heard the Miller ranch was raided," Josh

said softly. "Killed the parents and two kids. Also heard that the older girl got away, but they hadn't found her yet."

"Now they have, you might pass the word. Appreciate it, Josh, if you could take care of anything legal. Wills, any property she might now own. Probably nothing, unimproved homestead more than likely. Take care of it for me, will you."

"Be glad to, Captain. When she picks out what she wants, you take her on over to my place. Martha'll be glad to see both of you."

"If I'm going callin' you better put a new shirt and a hat on my tab too, Josh. How about that gray felt over there with the high crown. I might just trade you even up for an Indian pony that's tied up out in back of your door. You take the best one, the other one I'll donate to the U.S. Cavalry."

Josh nodded and watched Hannah. "Right pretty girl, Captain. You could do worse."

"Yes, a beautiful lady, Josh."

Josh chuckled and lifted the whiskey bottle. "One more for old times sakes, then I got to get to work."

Martha McCurdy had liked Hannah at once, and made like she was her own kin. Nothing would do but that Wade stay for supper. He hadn't been to see them for two years and he was long overdue for a good meal. Hannah had spent most of the afternoon in her room, crying, Chisholm guessed. But by supper time she came out dressed in a high buttoned frock, with ruffled sleeves and a waist that pinched in tightly. The print material brushed the floor as she walked.

After supper the women did the dishes, then Josh announced that he and Martha had to go back to the store to finish making up a new order for women's goods.

"You know I don't savvy none of them contraptions, Martha, and the stock is getting low. Now hush up and get your bonnet so we can get down there and get it done in a couple of hours."

Martha lifted her brows but said nothing as she and Josh went out, saying they would be back soon.

When they were gone, Chisholm stood and reached for his new hat. He suddenly felt uncomfortable.

"Well, I guess I better get going too."

"Wade, I don't want you to go. We need to have a talk. First about my family. I saw my parents killed. I'll never forget that, but what about my . . . my little sister and brother?"

"They didn't make it either, Hannah."

She blinked back tears. "I was afraid not." Tears came then, and she leaned against him. A couple of minutes later she dried her tears.

"But now life must go on, right? I remember my mama saying that when grandma died. Life must go on." She looked up at him. "Wade, I need you to help me once more."

"Yes, of course, anything I can do."

She stood and motioned for him to follow her. In her bedroom she turned down the lamp that had been left burning there, then she reached for Wade and put her arms around him, pressed her body firmly against him and kissed him hard on the mouth.

"Wade, don't you understand? I'll feel so much better if I can do this one small thing for you. Don't make me say anything else or do anything else. Help me, Wade. Please help me. Right now. Please!"

He bent and kissed her lips, then followed her as she sat on the side of the soft bed.

"Hannah. . . ."

She touched his lips with her fingers and caught his hand and brought it down on her breast.

"No more talk, Captain Chisholm. No more talk at all."

He sighed, kissed her again and rubbed her breast gently through the dress. Chisholm lay her down on the bed and leaned over her a moment, then he kissed her and his hands touched her and softly she responded with sounds and then soft moans of pleasure.

A half hour later she lay in his arms, still breathing heavily. She wouldn't let him undress her, only open the top of her dress and then pull up the long skirts. He had stripped off his pants, locked the bedroom door and then entered her gently. She had cried and then responded with such a display of rapture and delight that he had been totally surprised.

"Again, Wade?" she asked.

He laughed. "Not for a while — and anyway, I've got to get back to camp."

He came away from her slowly, then pulled on his pants and tucked in the new cotton plaid shirt. "I'll stop by the store and say good-bye to Josh. After he clears up any legal matters about your family, you probably should go on to Prescott. I've got some good friends there, and you'll need to get situated."

She smiled. "Wade Chisholm, you know I want to be with you. Don't you know that? I owe my life to you. Anything I do from now on will be for you. I have no other wishes. It was something I promised myself back in the cave, when you first spoke those words to me. I thought at first you were just another Indian . . . I thought. . . ."

"We'll talk about it later. Right now I've got another job to do. It's about those Apaches in the cave."

She suddenly looked worried, frightened. "Be careful, darling. I'd die now if anything happened to you, Wade Chisholm. You be careful."

He bent and kissed one of her breasts that still peeked through her open dress, then her lips. She sat up buttoning the fasteners, pulling down her skirts. Hannah blew out the kerosene lamp and they went to the front door. She kissed him again at the door, and then he put on his new felt hat with the high crown and walked out into the night.

Chisholm said his goodbyes to the Mc-Curdys, then made the short ride to the bivouac. If Major Black was still awake he'd make his report at once. He was sure the major would be up. From there on it would be up to the army, but Chisholm had an idea that they would be hearing the bugle call of "boots and saddles" very soon. A troop would ride into the Superstition

Mountains to confront the Apaches in their lair.

CHAPTER 9
ATTACK IN THE SUPERSTITIONS

It was nearly midnight. Major William Black had loosened the kerchief around his neck and blotted his forehead. It was still ridiculously hot inside the command tent where two kerosene lamps burned on the improvised table. The four officers on the campaign leaned over the table and studied the sketches Chisholm had made earlier.

The scout slouched in one of the folding chairs, a glass of sippin' whiskey in his hand, fatigue starting to tinge each word that he spoke. He had been up for forty-two hours without sleep and he was starting to unravel.

"And you say there is absolutely no way up from the bottom of the gorge to the cave," Major Black asked.

"Absolutely no way unless you're an ant, spider, or maybe a squirrel," Chisholm said.

"But attacking along this trail you describe would be suicide," Lieutenant Josh Donner said. "Two braves with rifles could hold off our whole force at any one of these bends in the trail along the face of the cliff."

"Not really," Black said. "The whole idea is to go in at night, silently, with surprise. So our force is positioned at the bend here, without being seen by the hostiles. It's even possible that we could send a team of sappers in close enough to throw dynamite charges into the cave itself, and force the hostiles out. If we had enough dynamite and could get a team below the parapet."

"Sir, I think I should tell you that we have only twenty sticks of dynamite with us. It was all that was in the entire camp at Prescott. The army can't get enough to meet the demand. As you know, dynamite is still a fairly new item in our supply system."

The speaker was Lieutenant John Burke, the supply officer — and the smartest of the junior officers under Black.

"Thank you, Lieutenant Burke, I realize that. I was dreaming. The idea of surprise still holds. With it we can bottle them up inside, force them to come out. What do you think, Chisholm?"

"Again, Major? Why don't we stow it for now and worry about it again in the morning. I'm talking in my sleep."

"One more time, Wade."

"The cave must have more than one

escape route. Those Chiricahuas can climb rocks like mountain goats. There may be a continuing trail up the other side of the cave — I didn't take time to check it out. Which means you can pin them down during the day, if you get in position at dawn, and that involves a night march and then a scramble down the trail. You can pin them down during the day, but at night they're going to filter out of there and get in positions to wipe out all of us come the dawn.

"So you have to split your forces and cover the top of the cliff, blasting away at everything that moves. You cover the far side trail if there's one and you try to move your sapper team in to blast the entrance of the cave. Unfortunately, the booze will all be gone long before we can get back there, so don't count on any more drunken parties. I was lucky on that one."

He stood, swayed, and Donner steadied him. "With the major's permission I'll leave the details to you, while I walk outside and collapse."

"Corporal!" Black called. A sleepy-eyed soldier came through the flap. "Escort Mr. Chisholm to Captain Thornton's tent and see that he gets blankets for the cot there." He turned to Chisholm. "Thanks, Wade, we'll see you tomorrow."

When he woke up just after the noon meal the following day, Chisholm found a sentry posted at the tent flap. The young man suggested Mr. Chisholm might want to eat at the officer's mess and then report to the major's tent.

Chisholm nodded. "Looks like things are happening around here, soldier."

"Yes, sir. We're about ready to move. A day, maybe two. I hear we're going right into the middle of the damn Superstition Mountains!"

"And you think that will be fun?" Chisholm asked, noting the excitement in the soldier's voice.

"Fun? Shooting Indians? Hell, I don't know, I've never done that before. But it sure will be a lot better than laying around here in this hot weather all the time."

The orders were drawn by the time Chisholm reached Black's tent. He was ushered inside and given a copy printed in block letters so there could be no mistake:

"Orders to Assault Chiricahua Apache stronghold in the Superstition Mountains: Drawn by: Major William H. Black, Commanding Officer, 5th U.S. Cavalry.

"August 14, 1872. Move entire base camp

to foot of Superstition Mounains near Salt River Canyon. Troops rest for remainder of day and following.

August 15: At dusk this day a force of 200 cavalrymen on foot to move into Superstition Mountains under the direction of Scout Wade Chisholm, and to approach the hidden cave of the Chiricahua. March to be made silently with the hope of surprise. Troopers will wear Indian-type moccasins to reduce noise and increase chance of surprise. To be in position on upper trail by midnight.

"August 16: As situation demands, to descend trail to cave in darkness beginning at 0100 hours and to be in position just before daylight, this date.

"Engage the enemy, pinning him within the cavern and demanding surrender. If no surrender is obtained, and no victory assured, to take blocking action before dusk.

"August 16: Dusk. To position a line of troopers on crest of bluff over cave, and at such places, ravines, draws, leading up from the 700 foot level where hostiles might attempt to escape their cave fortress. To engage any hostiles who try for such an exit.

"August 17: If, before dawn on the 17th, there is no victory, or containment, the forces shall be withdrawn to safer positions than those on the gorge trail and at the trail mouth. Defensive positions shall be dug or erected, and such forces as are on the trail to be added to the containment forces in an effort to isolate and capture the hostiles."

When Chisholm finished reading the orders, he looked up at Major Black. The other officers had left the room.

"As our scout, what do you think of the general plan of attack?" Black asked, relieving Chisholm of the operations order.

Chisholm allowed himself a small grin. "You seem to have covered all the bases. You've used the information I brought back."

"And tactically?"

"A scout has nothing to do with tactics, Major, especially to offer advice to the operations commander."

"True, but as an ex-captain with Indian fighting experience who has been over the ground involved, you become more than simply a scout. I'd be a fool not to ask for your advice."

Wade Chisholm grinned. About half of the officers he worked for eventually got around to making that little speech.

"It all depends on the situation and the terrain. If all goes well, it should work. We probably won't drive the Apaches out of the cave, and we sure won't starve them out. At least we'll know where they are, and how to get to them, which will mean that they will be forced to change their hiding spot. I doubt if they will find another one this good."

"You're saying that we should win the battle but not the war?"

"Right. And against the Apache, that's not half bad."

"Oh. Well, we'll see. I've heard from Prescott. Captain Thornton has taken his situation all the way to General Crook, throwing around counter charges against me, you, and Lieutenant Donner. A hearing has been scheduled for two weeks from today. I hope you'll be able to be in Prescott with the rest of us. We've all been called to testify."

"Crook will never let it go into the hearing."

"He's approved it so far. I think he's heard something about the good captain's record — and something from Swallow River Camp."

"Let's hope so. Anything else? I'm about to go find myself a piece of the Salt River that has some water in it and have myself a real bath."

"That's all, Chisholm. Oh, I like the new

color of your hair. Think it will ever wash clean?"

"About July of next year," Chisholm said as he went out the tent flap.

The two-hundred man column near Phoenix left on the usual trail march time, six a.m. The entire camp was in the procession with supply wagons, mules, extra mounts, and two hundred mounted and fully equipped cavalrymen and officers of this detachment of the 5th U.S. Cavalry.

The march was uneventful, with the troop pulling into a dry wash a half mile from the mouth of the Salt River canyon where enough firewood was found to set up camp. The bivouac was established and guards posted. The men were fed a hot meal at noon, unusual on the trail, then ordered to rest for the next six hours. There would be a muster at 6:30 p.m. with each man ready for the trail with 140 rounds for his Springfield single shot carbine, and twenty-four rounds for his pistol. The sabres would be left at the bivouac. One ration of hardtack was to be issued to each trooper.

"Walking!" rumbled Sergeant Timothy Kelly. "What the hell you mean we're walking, Captain? I'm no damn foot soldier!"

Chisholm sat beside the weathered old

sergeant and chuckled.

"You'll be walking or crawling on this one, lad, whichever your stomach tells you to do. 'Tis a thousand feet down and that trail is less than six inches wide. The major figures if the fat old Apache squaws can go down the trail, a fat Irish sergeant should be able to make it too."

"I didn't sign on as no grubcracking infantryman," Kelly grumbled. "I ain't no footslogger. I got me enlistment papers to prove it."

Chisholm laughed and pulled his new felt hat down over his eyes. "Go tell it to the major," Chisholm said and closed his eyes. He could get in another half hour of sleep before they pulled out.

An hour later they were well into the Superstition Mountains. The officers knew what to expect, most of the men did not. The order was for every man to wear moccasins, but they found only twenty pair in the whole camp. Those moccasins were fitted to the first twenty men in the line of march, the sharpshooters and point men.

Chisholm led the line with Lieutenant Burke right behind him. Major Black was at the center of the column and Lieutenant Donner brought up the rear. The plan was to march into the mountains in an effort to surprise the Indians. No talking or smoking was permitted. Any bit of equipment that jangled was taped into silence. A certain kind of grimness settled over the men as they realized they were marching into action against the hostiles. No casual patrol where they might spot hostiles, this was a sure contact, a fight. The veterans took it in stride, but the young men and the unblooded kept looking up each ravine and gully.

They marched for three hours and were near the summit of the Salt River gorge bluffs. Chisholm had convinced the major of the logic in coming up this way to the slanting trail. They would have some room to deploy troops, move them around to the other side and directly on top of the ledge if need be.

At midnight all the troops were assembled in a two hundred yard area, and the officers conferred. Black waved in his scout for the talk.

"So far I don't think they know we're here," Chisholm said.

"Good," Black said. "I want you to take six men and Lieutenant Burke and scout down the trail to the place where the horses are. Estimate how many animals are there and guess if most of the ones are there you saw before. I want to know if the braves are in the cave or half of them out on a raid. If they are outside we'll need a good security force at our backs too."

Chisholm ran lightly along the trail forging ahead, his Spencer on his shoulder. He waited from time to time for the soldiers to catch up. Now he slid along the trail silently, rounded a bend, and came to the small flush of sparse grass and the spring where the horses were kept.

He stopped in surprise. He could smell half a dozen sweaty animals. By the time the lieutenant and his men crept into the spot, Chisholm had the figures for them.

Twelve of the horses were still wet with sweat. It must have been two raiding parties, and the mounts had been ridden hard. They hadn't been in the spring for more than an hour. Most of the braves should be in the cave. Burke sent word back by runner to the major and they waited for instructions.

Black figured that he had to attack at once, and at the same time cover the back trail. He sent a force of thirty men down to the valley and they set up a blocking force a half mile from the ponies.

At the same time he ordered a hundred

men forward to go down the cliff trail to the horses and instruct Burke to go on to the cave. He kept the rest of his troops in reserve.

The thin light of the mountain dawn filtered onto the upper mesa when the hundred men started down the cliff trail in single file. The wild stories of the six-inch wide shelf quickly vanished and they found the going wasn't so hard. Each man had to take his time and watch for loose rocks. In some places they guessed where the trail went because the wall vanished and there was a thirty foot wide gentle slope. In other areas there was only fourteen inches of trail along the upthrust of granite. Each soldier watched the trooper ahead of him, and moved slowly, carefully. Orders came down the line in a whisper from one man to the next.

When they were about half way down, the trail opened on one of the wider spots where the men could sit and rest. Burke didn't want them too tired or nervous when they came to the point where they contacted the Indians.

Chisholm scouted ahead and found nothing unusual. The troop caught up with him and then they forged on ahead. Burke took a dozen of his sharpshooters who wore moccasins and, with Chisholm, they went out in front as an advance unit. They picked their way down the narrowing trail behind Chisholm. After another twenty minutes of slow going, Chisholm held up his hand for the men to halt.

It was almost daylight now. Burke stood beside the scout. Chisholm motioned the officer forward and they edged around a bend in the trail.

"There it is, Lieutenant," Chisholm said.

Burke stared at the cave in surprise and a sense of growing excitement. He studied it for a few seconds.

"That parapet of rock, is it natural? What a fortress that place is. I couldn't have designed one any better."

There were fires at the entrance. Evidently the returning warriors had lighted cooking fires and now their women were preparing food for them for a celebration. There was singing and much shouting from the cave mouth. From their location, slightly above the cave, they could see more than a dozen Indians in the small area.

Burke signalled his marksmen to follow and they slid around the bend in the trail and positioned themselves along the trail behind boulders and rocks. They were now only forty yards from the cave. Each man was told in whispers to pick out a different brave as a target and they all would fire on command. Burke watched his men, and as he saw them all nod, he gave the order to fire.

Six of the warriors were fatally wounded in that first volley. There were screams of surprise, pain and terror from the cave mouth as the Indians scrambled and crawled into the mouth and behind the parapet out of the line of fire.

The single volley of a dozen shots reverberated through the barren rocky hills like a sound chamber and the reserve force above on the trail with Major Black heard it plainly. He ordered Lieutenant Masters to take the first forty men in line and go down the trail to reinforce Burke.

The snare had been sprung. The Indians now must be trapped in the cave until dark. There was no need to send out any more blocking or security parties. Black waited to hear word from the troops below.

As the first men from Master's detail came to reinforce the already overmanned slope, the Indians began returning fire. Since the troopers were well under protection behind rocks, there was little damage done by the hostile's fire, and Chisholm saw only one soldier wounded.

Now Black began moving the rest of his forces closer to the battle. As he did, one of his men saw an Indian racing up the seemingly unclimbable slopes of the mountain. He was far up the cliff, well out of effective carbine range. The Indian turned and gave a scream of defiance at the cavalrymen.

A blacksmith attached to the unit lifted his carbine and fired in frustration at the escaping brave. To his surprise, the round found its mark killing the Indian. It was a good omen for the entire mission.

Major Black held his men in two groups, one up forward with Burke, the other in the upper part of the trail where he was. He was satisfied that with the blocking force above there could be no escape and that the Indians could not mount an assault from the cave that could punch through the force. He ordered the front unit to hold fire and called on the Apaches to surrender.

Chisholm watched the little drama with a grin. From the cave came a chorus of derisive shouts and screams which Chisholm translated to the red-faced lieutenant. The Apaches derided the soldiers, calling them fools, children, and already dead men. They said that this day was the last on earth for all the roundeyes, and that by tomorrow their naked bodies would be thrown over the cliff into the canyon below where the crows, buzzards and worms would eat their flesh.

"Are they bluffing?" Burke asked.

Chisholm shook his head. "There's not a hell of a lot we can do to hurt them now, is there, Lieutenant? We can't storm the cave. They've got rifles and a perfect field of fire, and even if we get to that wall, it's ten feet straight up, which means ladders or a stack of bodies below. And at the top we meet arrows, knives, lances, rifle balls — not to mention Apache squaws."

Burke nodded. "Then after dark they start sneaking out of there and move up the slope to get us in their sights for the coming of daylight."

"About the size of it. Just about the way you boys figured it out a couple of days ago back at the bivouac."

"What we need is a new factor, a situation or terrain alteration that might change the picture," Burke said.

Major Black had also considered the possibilities. Now he again called on the Indians to surrender, telling them that they could send out their women and children first and they would not be harmed.

Again the Indians jeered at them and sent a blast of bullets into the trail.

The soldiers were given the order to return fire and for some minutes the barrage continued, but no one was hurt by the furious flying lead.

Chisholm had not been firing; instead, he was looking at the cave. Over the top of the parapet he could see a two-foot opening that showed the roof of the cave. It appeared to be solid granite. Chisholm used his Spencer repeater and put seven shots into the top of the cave and watched as the rounds all richocheted downward and *inside* the cave. Amid the firing he heard a howl of pain from the cave.

"Lieutenant, you might suggest to your men that they fire into the top of the cave, that two foot opening over the parapet. The rounds richochet downward into the cave and it should at least scare hell out of them. Anything else is wasted lead."

Burke had brought along a Springfield carbine for the fight and sent two shots into the cave roof. He turned, grinned, and passed the world along the line. Soon, every man who could see the spot was sending round after round into the roof of the cave where the lead slanted downward, and some rounds shattered and tore into the Apaches.

In a lull of firing they could hear the screams and cries of the braves and also of women and children.

The warriors ran forward to crouch directly behind the rock parapet at the front of the cave, but still they were being hit by the bounding lead.

"Cease fire!" Major Black called from the rear line of troops. Once more he asked the Apaches to surrender. There was no response. Then they heard the wailing chant of the Apache Death Song.

"Here they come!" a trooper on the first line shouted.

Twenty warriors leaped on top of the parapet firing rapidly. Ten more burst from the far side of the wall and ran low to the ground toward a jumble of rocks ten yards away.

"Now we've got some real trouble," Chisholm said as he began firing.

CHAPTER 10
MIRACLE FROM ABOVE

Chisholm heard new firing from above him and saw the second line of soldiers in back of them on the trail. Evidently, the braves in the cave hadn't seen the other troops, and figured they were going against the small group behind the lower rocks.

The initial barrage of carbine fire killed six of the charging hostiles, and stopped the rush, as the Indians who could, ran and limped back for the cave. Those still alive on the parapet tumbled inside the enclosure.

The firing into the top of the cave evidently had changed the hostiles' minds about waiting out the soldiers. Now they were faced with less than a safe haven.

Major Black ordered his men to concentrate the heaviest possible fire into the cave roof, and they would get ready to charge the stronghold under cover of the withering hail of lead. Black had worked forward in the line until he was at the head of it near the rocks, only forty yards from the cave. He conferred with Lieutenant Bush and Chisholm and they decided that half of the troopers would continue firing and the other half would cross in front of the parapet and strike the small entrance to the cave from which some of the Indians had charged. It would be a hazardous operation, but the officers felt it was the only way to bring victory, and that the risk was worth it.

Before the order to attack could be given, something happened to alter the major's plans.

The blocking detail of troopers on the trail out to the valley high on the top of the bluffs had heard the heavy firing in the gorge and at once moved up to the face of the dropoff to see if they could find out what was happening and to offer any assistance if possible. Peering over the chasm they found that they were directly over the cave, and saw in a moment the situation: the hostiles huddled behind the parapet for protection and the lines of bluecoats on the trail leading down toward the cave.

Sergeant Timothy Kelly had been in charge of the blocking detail, and now he stared below and saw the problem. The Indians were in a perfect defensive position and it would be costly in cavalry blood to root them out. He kicked in frustration at one of the rocks at his feet and then stared down at it. There were hundreds of the rocks, six to eight inches in diameter, lying on top of the cliff. He looked over the side, then moved twenty yards to one side on the top of the bluff and called his troopers around him.

"We've got a surprise for those damned savages below, boys. Gather up as many of these small rocks as you can and bring them right here. Move it, we've got no time to waste!"

Five minutes later the twenty men had more than two hundred rocks in a pile.

"Get ready, men," Kelly said. "On my signal we line up along the edge and start dropping these rocks directly into that open spot in front of the cave and on that rock wall too. We'll fill up the cave if we have to. Ready . . . now!"

Below, near the cave, Chisholm checked the half of the troop who fired at the cave mouth. He could hear the wails and screams of the hostiles through the carbine fire. Major Black had briefed the squad leaders and the other half of his troop crouched behind rocks waiting for the bugle call to send them dashing toward the cave.

Without warning, rocks began falling on

the parapet and the front of the cave. Chisholm looked upward and saw at the top of the cliffs blue-shirted figures dripping the rocks over the side.

"Major, look up there," Chisholm shouted pointing upward. "We don't need an assault, we've got a crew at work with man's oldest weapon."

Some of the stones shattered when they struck the rock wall and the other rocks below sending fragments slamming into the cave like bullets. The rocks falling five-hundred feet straight down gained tremendous speed, and when they hit the scrambling Apaches, they tore off limbs, splattered torsos and smashed bodies into unrecognizable shapes. Some of the rocks bounced off the parapet and went careening over the side another seven hundred feet into the river below.

The roar and crashing of the rocks hitting the cave soon drowned out everything else, including the carbine fire.

It seemed like an eternity that the stones fell, but Chisholm figured it was only two or three minutes that the terror rained down on the hapless Chiricahua. When they stopped, only the dust remained and an ominous silence. The guns had ceased firing now, too, not on command, but simply because the men were in awe of the destruction the rocks were doing. Men and officers alike stared at the dust as it hung over the cave like a shroud. Then it was whipped away by the ever-present winds. Even the death song chanting inside the cave had stopped.

Major Black stood on the trail and bellowed his orders.

"Charge and secure the cave!" he thundered. The sixty men primed to make the assault swept across the few remaining yards and surged into the cave.

Not a shot or a shout came from the dazed and stricken Indians. Chisholm went inside with the first few men and, at the entrance, he faced a horrible sight: crushed bodies littered the exterior shelf where the braves had been caught clustered behind the parapet. Some of the bodies were hardly recognizable as men. Scores of Apaches were dead or dying, more than half of them women and children. Arms and legs stuck from piles of the rocks which had rained down on them, and from small rock slides some of them had caused.

Major Black leaned against the parapet breathing heavily. He yelled for Burke.

"Disarm any braves still able to fight. Then see what you can do to save any of those not already dead. Get the living out of here and on the trail. Take any able to walk back up the trail and hold them at the pasture." He shook his head. "My God, I've seen battles, but nothing like this, not ever!"

Later a count came down as Black and Chisholm stood outside the cave staring at the bodies carried past.

"Sir, there are seventy-six Apache dead. We have confiscated eighty-seven rifles and carbines and thirty-four hand guns. As near as I can tell there are thirty-seven Chiricahua still alive, but at least half of those are so badly wounded they can't stand to be moved to the valley."

"Thank you, Lieutenant Burke. And our own casualties?"

"Three, sir. Two troopers suffered minor bullet wounds and a third broke his leg in the charge. All three have been treated and are in the pasture."

"Very good. Now, how much longer will it take you here?"

"Sir . . . ?"

"To bury the dead."

Chisholm cleared his throat and motioned to the major.

"Sir, I would suggest to the major that the Apaches should not be buried. It's against their beliefs. They would rather be left in the open or taken to the top of the cliff. In the open their spirits can be free to soar into the heavens. Don't put them underground, that would be a terrible fate for them."

Black stared at Chisholm for a moment, then nodded. "Yes, I had heard that." He turned to Burke. "Leave the dead where they have fallen, Lieutenant. I want to be ready to move out of here in half an hour. We'll have to carry the wounded. Don't leave any Apache who is still alive behind."

By the time the last of the troopers marched to the small pasture above on the trail, three more of the Apaches had died and their bodies had been left on the trail. At the pasture the troops ate their hardtack and drank the spring dry, each new group waiting for the small pool to fill before the men drank.

By noon, eight more wounded Indians had died. Chisholm refused to look at any more of the band closely. He had already recognized several of the dead as those he had known when he was growing up, and he didn't want to see any more.

They waited until darkness and then were ordered to sleep for the night. Sergeant Kelly had brought back his men from the cliff and had been openly congratulated by Major Black.

Chisholm didn't sleep at all that night. The wailing and chanting for the dead by the living Apaches filled the darkness and kept many of the troopers awake. But the major looked at Chisholm and then ordered that the Chiricahua not be stopped. It was their right to mourn their dead.

First call the next morning on the bugle sounded at exactly 4:45 a.m. At least half of the troops were already awake and had rolled their blankets, anxious to march.

Major Black made an inspection of the prisoners. There were now only eighteen captives left alive; all but one of them were wounded in some way: two braves, ten squaws, six children.

The prisoners were instructed by Chisholm that they must do as the soldiers commanded. Most were still dazed by the slaughter in the cave and at losing entire families to the smashing rocks.

The Apaches were placed alternately between troopers in the center of the line of march. The trooper behind each Apache was held responsible for that prisoner. If the captive tried to escape, the trooper would chase him and shoot only if there was a danger the prisoner might get away.

During the eight-mile march back to the camp at the foot of the Superstition Mountains, none of the Apaches tried to escape. When they got back to the bivouac, Black called Chisholm to his tent and offered him a glass of whiskey. As the two men settled back, the major spoke freely.

"Chisholm, it's a damned waste, having you out of uniform. I've sent a request to General Crook to look with favor on your application for reenlistment at your former rank. Dammit, Chisholm, we need men with your experience and your understanding of the Indians. We must have more men with your insights and knowledge if we're ever going to make this Arizona Territory safe for the white settlers. And the people are coming, thousands of them. Some day that little village of Phoenix may be as big as Prescott, and perhaps ten times larger. I don't want your answer right now about reenlisting. Just think about it. Consider it as a possibility, that's all I ask."

Chisholm smiled. It wasn't the first time he had been approached about such an idea.

"Yes, Major, I'll certainly consider it. I understand you're giving the men a day's rest before starting out for Prescott. If that's the case, I'd like to be relieved of duty to go back to Phoenix."

"Oh, yes, the girl. They tell me she is a pretty lady."

"Yes, you might say that. Josh McCurdy is working out her business there, to see if there's anything left at the homestead or any other property. I want to check it out and then see that she gets to Prescott where she is to stay with some friends until she can get situated."

Black smiled. "Yes, I understand, Chisholm. Consider it a week's leave for a job well done. I'm sure General Crook is going to be delighted with your work these last few days. I'll want your final report and to see you back at Prescott when you get in. From what you've told me, this could be the one stroke we needed to break the power of the Chiricahua in this area. Of course we've still got the rest of the Apache bands, the Mescaleros, the Coyoteros, and four or five more. But it's a fine start. I think the settlers around here can relax a bit."

"Yes, sir. I hope so. Now, sir. If I have your permission, I'll be riding out for Phoenix."

"Right, Chisholm. I'll see you in Prescott."

CHAPTER 11
GENERAL GEORGE F. CROOK, COMMANDING

Chisholm stopped at the general store when he got to Phoenix and tied his army mount at the hitching rail in front. He stomped some of the trail dust off his boots and pounded it away from his gray shirt and hat before he went inside.

As he reached for the door it swung open. He saw a blur of blue dress, long brown hair, and a radiant face, then she was in his arms, hugging him tightly, holding him like she would never let go. A moment later she let loose and spun away, showing him her new dress, light brown eyes sparking in her scrubbed face.

"Like it?" she asked.

Chisholm laughed softly. "Yes, Hannah, of course I like it. You're beautiful." He caught her hand and led her to the back of the store. "Why are you here?"

"I'm working here, isn't that grand? Mr. McCurdy said I could look after all of the clothes and notions and things, even some of the groceries. I'm having the best time in all my life."

Josh McCurdy came in from the back. "Well now, and if it isn't the wee soldier boy who has come back from the wars. Sure and you're still in one chunk, lad?"

"Aye, that I am," Chisholm said, dropping naturally into the heavy Irish brogue he had heard from his thirteenth year. "But what in tarnation is this about putting the wee lass here to doing manual labor?"

"Now, you're jesting, boy, for sure. She's a bright girl, does her sums better than me, and pretty too. There's another store going up and I don't like the competition, so I hired the prettiest lass in the whole of Arizona. Smart idea?"

"If she wants to work."

"And that's not all that's been happening around here," Hannah said, then paused. A hint of a frown shaded her face. "Oh, I forgot — the Indians, the cave, did you. . . ."

"Yes, Hannah, we found them, and the Chiricahua will never be a threat to the people of Arizona again, at least not for a long, long time. Now. What's your other news?"

She kept looking at him, remembering that terrible afternoon her parents died, and the long trip to the mountains. "Did a lot of them . . . die?"

"Yes, a lot. Now. Your news, what is your big news?"

"Oh, yes." The frown was gone, her pretty face changing into a smile. "Mr. McCurdy went out to the folks' homestead to see if anything was left and he talked to some neighbors. One of them found some things that hadn't been burned. There was an old trunk and inside was a cash box with four hundred dollars in gold coins. So I'm a rich woman!"

"A little rich, but not as rich as you were," Josh said.

"Oh, well. I didn't know what else to do with all that money, so I spent two hundred dollars and I bought a little house right here in Phoenix. It's just a short way from Aunt Martha, and she helped me put up curtains and I've got one braided rug and she helped me get settled. There's a wood stove and a big living room and a bedroom and a kitchen!"

Chisholm sat on the small counter and looked at the girl in surprise.

"Now why did you go and do that? You've got no roots here. I thought you'd be going to Prescott or maybe Denver."

"No. No, I want to stay right here. I mean,

I think my parents would have wanted me to. They came out here because they thought this was good country and would be great some day. And now I have a job and Mr. McCurdy says the town is growing, a new store going up, and there's a blacksmith now in town, and the hotel, and two more houses started up last week with lumber hauled in. Aunt Martha says it's a good idea to stay here. And besides. . . ."

"But a house? How old are you, eighteen? You legally can't even own property yet."

"Well . . . Mr. McCurdy can, and he helped me with the papers. His name is on them, but it's mine when I get to be twenty-one . . . or I get married."

"Thanks, Josh, you really helped matters didn't you?"

The small Irishman snorted. "Sure and I know what I'm doing, even if some folks don't. *Some people* don't know a good thing when they see it, when it's pushed at them like a bowl full of cherries. Time was when a good Irishman knew his mind and struck out to get what he wanted. And ye be what twenty-four or twenty-five years now? You're past due to take a wife, lad. Sure and it would settle you down some. I've had my say." He went into the back room of the store and slammed the door.

Hannah stood watching Chisholm. She wanted to rush over and kiss him and hold him so tightly, but somehow she knew this wasn't the right time. She looked at him closely, then sighed.

The sound seemed to bring him to life. He walked to her and kissed her lips, putting his arms around her gently, holding her. She smiled and kissed him back lightly.

"I never thought you were going to do that. Wade, don't pay any attention to what Mr. McCurdy said. I bought the house because I wanted to make it easier for us to be together. Now you can come anytime. I just want to be with you. Wade, you don't have to marry me. I told you that. I want you and I never want to be away from you."

He let go of her, held up one finger for silence, then left her and went into the store's back room.

Josh sat on a packing box looking through some goods he had received.

"Well, is it all settled?"

"Nothing is settled except that you're a meddler, Josh." Chisholm stared at the merchant sternly, then grinned and grabbed his hand. "And I thank you for everything you've done for Hannah. You never can tell, I might just marry that girl eventually, but I've only known her for five days."

"That's all I ask. Hannah can be a persuasive woman, I've found that out these past few days."

"Agreed. Now, I'm going over to the hotel and buy myself a hot tub and a long sleep, then I'll come back and we'll talk turkey. You really can't afford to hire Hannah and pay her. Not enough for her to keep up a home."

"Well, I'll manage, and we can talk about that later," Josh said.

In the main part of the store, Chisholm told the girl he was going to get a room at the hotel and a hot tub bath. Before he could finish, she broke in to ask him to come over to her new house for supper.

"About seven o'clock. We'll have a fashionably late supper, and you can have a guided tour of my new house and lot."

She would not hear of any excuses as she led him to the door, gave him his hat, and said goodbye. Outside, Wade wasn't sure if he liked this turn of events. Somehow, whenever he brushed against women lately things seemed to get out of step, to richochet off in some strange direction. He sighed and went for his bath in the New Phoenix hotel.

About six o'clock, Chisholm went back to

the store and bought a new pair of "dress up" pants and a shirt, changing into them in the back room. Then with Josh's directions, he rode over to the new house. It was a small frame affair that a widower sold because he wanted to go back to Denver. The outside was painted white with a blue trim, and like all the other yards in Phoenix the desert ground was barren with no grass or flowers. Here and there, however, a small cactus gave life to the terrain.

He knocked on the front door and Hannah opened it. She had on a different dress, had curled the ends of her long hair and brushed it until it shone and tumbled like a brown torrent down her shoulders. She smiled, brown eyes sparkling with excitement.

"Look, isn't it wonderful! My very first house. My own home! Come in, Wade," she bubbled, putting her hand in his.

He stepped inside, closed the door, and sniffed.

"That can't be. . . . Is that what I think it is you're cooking . . . corned beef and cabbage?"

She nodded, too excited to say a word.

"Good Lord, woman. How did you learn so quickly?" He scooped her up and carried her to the small kitchen where the Franklin wood stove's heat bubbled the cabbage in an iron pot on the front lid. Chisholm set her down in the kitchen and tasted the cabbage, then yelped in delight and kissed Hannah. "You keep cooking like that and some Irishman is going to come along and snap you up for his bride."

"Anyone I know?" she asked.

"That's what we're going to have a long talk about. Tomorrow I leave for Prescott to make out my final report on the scouting mission."

"But that's tomorrow. You'll be here tonight."

"Yes, Hannah, I'll be here tonight."

"Good, perfect!"

The next morning she insisted on packing him a dinner. He told her he'd be riding thirty miles to the Henshaw ranch and staying overnight there. Then it was another easy thirty miles on into Prescott. He should arrive about the same time the troopers did.

Hannah had kissed him gently as he left.

"Remember, Wade Chisholm, I want you back here. You can come anytime you want to and stay as long as you like. I'd be more than happy to marry you if you ask. But I know I owe my life to you, so anything I can ever do. . . ."

He kissed her again, said he'd be back within a week, and then rode into the fresh morning light.

The two hundred troopers and officers of the Apache patrol arrived at Camp Prescott four hours before the scout did. Word had spread through the camp quickly about the smashing victory at the Salt River gorge cave. When Chisholm rode past the gates, he was asked to report at once to the commanding officer.

Chisholm left the mount and his bedroll with a corporal at the stables and brushed as much of the trail dust off his clothes as he could. Then carrying his new felt hat, he went to the base commander's office. A first sergeant saw him coming, stared at his brown-reddish hair, then told him to go in and see Major Black. The major was staring out a window when Wade came in.

"Well, Chisholm, you made good time. I didn't expect you for a week yet."

"My business in Phoenix ended earlier than I expected, Major."

"So I see. Well, let's get to it. Colonel Crook said he wanted to see you the minute you came on the post."

Major Black led the way down a corridor and to the end corner room of the frame building. There was a carpet on the floor, a massive oak desk facing the door, and behind it stood Lieutenant Colonel George F. Crook, Commander of the Army's Department of Arizona.

As soon as Chisholm came in the room, Crook moved over and shook his hand.

"Congratulations, Wade. It looks like you have done it again. Your good scout work and some lucky cannonading with boulders has won the day."

"We were lucky, sir. Major Black had us at the right place at the right time."

Crook laughed, preening his moustache and full beard. "Wade, you always were a diplomat. Black has already told me what you did. Without you there would have been no attack, let alone a victory." He went back to his desk and sat. "I'll expect your written report on the patrol tomorrow."

"You'll have it, General."

"Wade, a man is what the paymaster counts out to him each month. He calls me a lieutenant colonel, that's what I 'm."

"You'll always be a major general to me, sir," Wade said. "And I hope you get your stars back very soon."

"Wade, I need to have another little talk with you. Would you excuse us, Major?"

Major Black stood, saluted smartly, got a

176

nod from Crook, then went out, closing the door softly.

Crook tossed Wade a cigar, then a round-packet of sulphur matches pasted together they called "stinkers." Chisholm bit off the end of the stogie, tore one of the stinkers off the pack and lit the cigar. When he had puffed a few times, Crook motioned for him to sit down. The two men looked at each other.

"You're just as tough, as mean, as ornery, and as brilliant as ever, you know that, Wade?"

"You missed all my bad points, George."

"True, but we both know them. Wade, I'm delighted with this patrol. From what I can see, the Chiricahua Apaches really won't be able to bother the settlers for a hundred years."

"And the Chiricahua nation will curse the day I was born," Chisholm said grimly. "Some of the prisoners recognized me, even in my shirt and hat. They tried to spit on me. The word will be all over the Apache nation within a week."

"You made your decision about that a long time ago, son. It got a lot more personal this past few days." His features softened. "Wade, I know how you feel. Some of those people killed out there were your blood relatives. I understand that and I realize you know this is something that must happen when our two cultures collide this way. But we can do everything possible to make the collision as friendly and as bloodless as possible.

"As you know, there are more Apaches in the Superstitions. I'm not sure if they are Coyoteros or Jicarilla. But from what I've heard this band is at least thinking about coming out peacefully and going to the reservation. It shouldn't be a fight. But I need someone who can go in and talk to them. You're the best man for the job."

"I'd have to think about it."

Crook had been prepared for this. He tossed an object to Chisholm who caught it and looked in his hand. There lay a gold oak leaf, the mark of the rank of major.

"That's yours, *if* you'll sign up again. I've got special orders from General Sherman this week. It will be a permanent rank, and your commission reactivated. That other thing two years ago is long forgotten." Crook stroked his forked beard and heavy moustache while he watched Chisholm.

Before either of them could comment the door burst open and Captain Arthur J. Thornton strode into the room. He was in full dress uniform. He saw Wade sitting, smoking a cigar, and his agitated face seemed to billow with angry blood. He stood ramrod stiff in front of the desk.

"General, sir. The Apache patrol is back. I demand an immediate hearing. I demand, sir, that I be allowed to clear myself."

"Captain, you are restricted to your quarters. You shouldn't be here. Return to your quarters at once, sir."

"But sir, the perpetrators of this slander are here. You can understand my. . . ." He turned and stared at Chisholm. "Liars. They're all liars, sir. Even our own Army men. And Chisholm, that bastard civilian! It's all his fault. He goaded that young Donner into it." Thornton's eyes flamed with fury as he reached for his pistol but it wasn't in his belt. Then he grabbed his sabre and drew it, lunging at Chisholm, who kicked the chair over springing backwards. He caught a heavy cushion and charged the hysterical captain who made a lunge with the sabre, impaling it in the cushion. At the same moment Chisholm jerked the pillow to one side, ripping the blade from the frantic man's hands.

When Thornton looked up at Chisholm he stared into the barrel of the scout's .44. He could see that all six chambers were filled with ugly, deadly lead bullets.

"Guard!" Crook called. Two men ran into the room. "Confine the captain to his quarters. Lock him in."

Thornton lost all of his fight. He slumped against the guards and they led him away.

When he was gone and the door closed, Chisholm straightened the chair and pulled the sabre from the pillow. "Afraid we ruined the cushion, sir. What will happen to Thornton?"

"I had already decided. I've been over all the evidence and the statements. I've also talked to some of the enlisted men who were at Swallow River camp. The captain has some serious mental problems when it comes to combat. I'll convince him to resign his commission and then all charges against him will be dropped. It shouldn't be too hard to convince him, since now he has an attempted murder charge as well. He'll go back to Boston where his father owns a bank. He'll make a good banker. Consider the case of Captain Thornton closed. Now, what about the oak leaves?"

Chisholm held up the gold indicator of rank and smiled. Then he tossed it back to Crook.

"Not right yet, General. Maybe in a year. There's still too many hard feelings in the army. You know the stories. I might think about going into the Superstitions again for you. If I do, the Coyoteros will know about Salt River gorge. It will be a fight for me. Give me a month or so before you ask me again. Anyway, it will be cooler in the fall for all of your new men." He stood.

"Where to now, Wade? I was hoping you might go along with me on some hunting."

"I'm afraid not. I have another small problem back at Phoenix that I'm going to have to spend some time with and see if I can figure it out."

Lt. Col. George F. Crook smiled. "Yes, I've heard about that problem. I would say you'll enjoy it whichever way it goes. I've always been partial to brown-haired women myself."

Chisholm laughed, stood and saluted smartly. He received a smile and a precise military salute from Crook. Then Chisholm did a military about-face and marched out the door.

For some strange reason he was anxious to be on the move again. He would find some paper and write out his report, quick, clear, and to the point. Then he would be on his way back to Phoenix first thing in the morning. He would find time for a few drinks with Sergeant Kelly and they would tell lies until the small hours of the night.

Then Phoenix. There might even be some more corned beef and cabbage left. And he would have to decide something about the cook. It would take him at least a month to do that. The more he thought about the cook, the broader his smile became.

The employees of Thorndike Press hope you have enjoyed this Large Print book. All our Thorndike and Wheeler Large Print titles are designed for easy reading, and all our books are made to last. Other Thorndike Press Large Print books are available at your library, through selected bookstores, or directly from us.

For information about titles, please call:

(800) 223-1244

or visit our Web site at:

www.gale.com/thorndike
www.gale.com/wheeler

To share your comments, please write:

Publisher
Thorndike Press
295 Kennedy Memorial Drive
Waterville, ME 04901